Gloriana G. Selvanathan LTCL a post graduate was born in Sri Lanka and living in Berlin for the past twenty years was a radio artiste as a singer, radio actor, editor and translated books for Back to the Bible Broadcast in Sri Lanka. A TV presenter, documentary producer and a journalist for film festivals and teaches English in Berlin. She is the representative for Trinity College London in Berlin, and for the second year will be the jury for the Film Festival (International) in Chennai, India. She is a gold medallist for Best Short Story 2000. Writing a novel is only a desire for her.

Fourth dimension of love

By

Gloriana G. Selvanathan

Published 2005 by arima publishing

www.arimapublishing.com

ISBN 1-84549-032-0

Printed and bound in the United Kingdom

Typeset in Garamond 11/14

arima publishing
ASK House, Northgate Avenue
Bury St Edmunds, Suffolk IP32 6BB
t: (+44) 01284 700321

www.arimapublishing.com

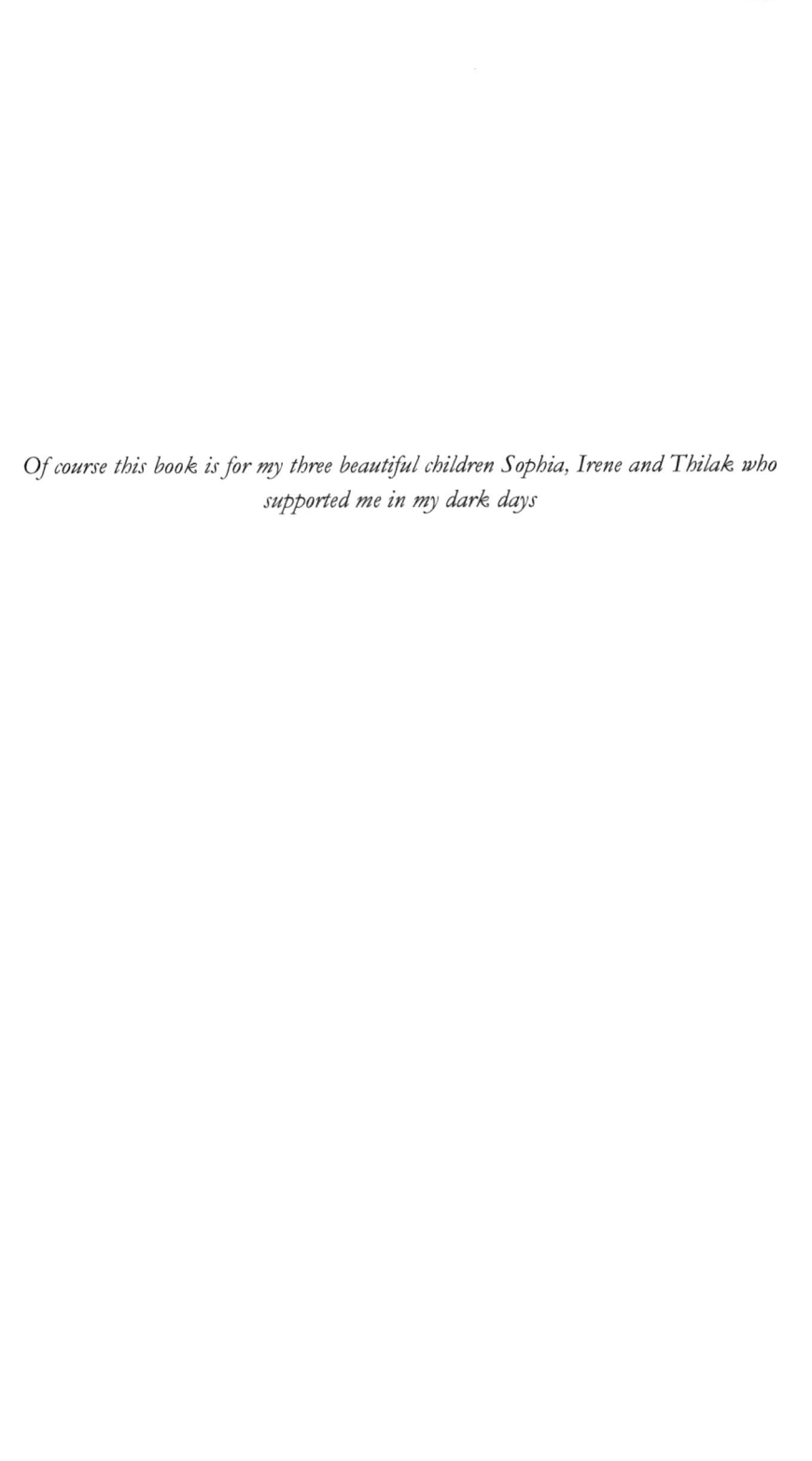

Of course this book is for my three beautiful children Sophia, Irene and Thilak who supported me in my dark days

Chapter 1

The advertisement on the paper was a god sent proposition for Valerie. 'Not doing anything was the biggest strain' she thought. She was on the verge of booking a flight to go anywhere in the world in order to get away from the present depression she was under going. But she was gratified to have discovered the scepticism that had seeped to warn her that going away was not going to solve her problem in the long run. She refused to be placated by any earthly excuses. May be she would have been more depressed when there was no one like her father to talk to. Thinking of her father brought a profound gleam on her face which was seldom these days. Had it not been for him she would have continued the impulse of not believing in justice. She made no attempt to hide her feelings. But this was one point in her life where she was going to make her own decision and face the consequence. She was old enough to do that. The dark lines on that determined face was the tell tale sign of the adversaries of the recent past. Losing one's job was not something new in the twenty first century (only getting one). There could be thousands of reasons to lose the job but false accusation should not be one of them. In Valerie's case, resistance was futile. The moral cowardice on the part of the authorities forced her to make a decision against her will. She had to resign in the eyes of the public as a misfit in the media. That was her frustration. Now this job gave a twinge of hope to restart her career and a new life in a new country with new people, 'Provided I get the job' whispered her inner mind. Without any further contemplation she sat down to formulate her application.

By the time Valerie was satisfied with her draft there were signs of relief on her otherwise beautiful face. She heard a car coming and she lifted her head to see her father's convertible rounding the porch of their house. Quickly she bundled everything together and stuck them in one of the drawers of her desk. She could not give a plausible reason for this action. She was acting like a child. But recently, the absence of sense had made it easy for her to show that calm and impersonal behaviour. She was no more the same pleasant person she used to be. She hated discussing her future plans with anyone including her dearest father, who was puzzled but willing to help her.

'I could take it to the post when I go for my walk in the morning' she thought closing the drawer. There was a kind of determination on her face, firm and fixed. She knew that nothing was difficult as long as one knew how to go forward.

****

"The golden reflection of the sun, the silvery touch of the moon, a drifting boat by a gentle breeze"... someone was reading a story on the radio when Valerie woke up the next morning. She was sitting up on her bed, trying to grasp the situation. The automatic setting in her radio had begun its service as usual. For a moment she thought she was late and had to hurry up and then she realised it was weeks since she had lost her job. Not only today, but for the days to come she need not hurry. And driving through the hustle and bustle of the crowded London streets sounded like a dream of the past more than reality. Even now the memory of her exciting career lingered at the back of her mind, giving her heart a twist with pain.

Stirred by the warmth of the sun she got up and entered her bathroom. There was a smell of fresh lavender coming through the window. She allowed the bath to run and then took the brush to clean her teeth. They were one of her most unique features. That smile of hers had captured many viewers that she was approached by tooth paste firms for advertisements. Only her contract with her company prevented her from doing that. "What's the use" she sighed. While brushing she looked at the heart shaped face that reflected on the mirror. "When did I get that melancholy look on my face? Don't I look like a stranger, or rather like a battered poor devil?" She knew she was being too hard on herself. The drastic change was not only in her appearance but also in her otherwise peaceful life. The restlessness, the irritation, the anxiety, the detachment to life, the loss of hope, and losing faith in herself and in others - a train of negative aspects were sinking and floating in an irregular pattern, without giving her the slightest chance what to make out of them. A slow motion of agony gripped her heart.

Through the mirror she could see the bath filling. Closing the tap she added some more bath salt before dropping the towel down and getting into the bath tub. Her foot measured the warmth of the water and she slowly immersed herself in it, the lather covering her body. Gradually her whole body vanished into the water up to the neck. She closed her eyes and she felt relaxed both in body and soul. But she couldn't help herself thinking about those horrible experiences she encountered during the past weeks that changed her life.

****

Valerie was enjoying a walk from the parking lot to her office across the street. It was a small building complex. She took out the ID and looked. VALERIE WILSON, Senior Production/Marketing Assistant. Yes, that was she at the local television company. 'HOYDI TV' was the channel. The name sounded a bit funny, but it was chosen according to the numerology they said, by Harold the boss, and no one knew the rest. Well it sounded like one of those modern names of the migrant Asians which had complicated phonetic sounds without any meaning. There were many stories behind the name. One of them was that Harold Winslow, the founder, had had an Indian sweetheart. She had chosen the name and then she left him when they had a difference of opinion about morals in life. He did not change the name when it gathered momentum on the market.

At twenty six Valerie was an elegant brunette with wide black eyes and long hair, with a skin that was simply out of the world, a sure inheritance from her Spanish grandmother. Above all the innocent eyes and the slight jerk she gave when she walked, always turned a few heads when she walked around the London streets. Her taste in dresses and colours was unique. At the studio almost all the men, except the big boss and his business partner who were suspected to be having a secret relationship, (well it was no more a taboo after the state accepted gay marriages), the rest of them tried to flirt with her outrageously without any success. The best were already married or too old and the rest only hoped. The vitality of her body the vigour in her speech, the lingering smile, the slightly tilted chin, the natural flush adding colour to the heart shaped face, the beautiful tan of her skin, the half opened sensuous lips, the slender sexy legs and the best of all, the expressive floating eyes were some of 'the gifts god had given to her' or rather that was what she said when someone made a comment on any one of them. Nobody at the office refused any thing when she turned her appealing eyes towards them. No, not flirting but simply mesmerising them.

Today she was wearing a pale blue two piece, her hair was in a half tied half hanging casual style and her mouth was painted with a slight touch of lipstick. Her face was almost free of makeup except for the eyes which were discreetly made up that one could never guess.

"Good morning Charles" she greeted the guard as she entered the building.

"Good morning miss," he continued "We've got sunshine today, and you look great as ever" He was old enough to be her father. "Thank you" she emphasised the 'you' as though this was the first time she was hearing a complement. The automatic swing doors opened as she stepped into the lobby.

Hanna was at the reception. "Good morning Miss Valerie" she always dropped the surnames. It was a privilege she took with younger people. "Good morning Hanna" Valerie hated unnecessary formalities. She pressed the button for the lift. It was then that she had the uneasy feeling she got before something terrible happened. Valerie wanted to ignore it but the feeling was strong. The right hand and the shoulder were twitching in a peculiar way. She had it just before her mother died, and on many other occasions like when she failed her first audition in singing, and when she lost one of her friends in an accident. And at times Valerie admitted to being superstitious, the 'Spanish gene' she said. Before she could think further the lift opened and she got in and pressed number four. The lift smelt of cigar, the one that you get when Mr. Winslow was around. 'So the Big bad wolf is early today' was the last thought in her mind when she emerged out of the lift and headed towards the office.

As she was signing the register, a voice whispered close to her ears "Valerie come to my room. I would like to have a word with you." If it had been anybody else she would have given them a piece of her mind regarding manners. Unfortunately it was Mr. Winslow, her boss, so she only nodded her head and at the same time said "Yes, Mr. Winslow." She winked at Mark who was waiting to sign and followed her boss.

HW himself was a puny little man, always fully dressed. Nobody could guess his age, because he dyed his hair allowing a little grey on the sides. He looked like one of those villains from the Hindi films, so thoroughly artificial. The only appealing feature was his hooked nose. Otherwise he had scar like marks on his face making people to wonder how he managed to shave on that uneven surface. If he turned his revolving chair to face the wall no one would know he was present except for the puffs from his cigar. He was selfish, unscrupulous and ambitious. On the whole he was a typical business man suitable for this wicked world. His personal life was more complicated. He lived alone in the suburbs of London. He never invited his staff to his house therefore nobody knew how he lived. Then there was a sudden change. It all started when Alen became a partner some years ago. Slowly HW's affinity with men surfaced. Eye brows were raised at first, with secret exchange of glances which were reduced to meaningful smiles. A transparent cloud of euphemism always surrounded such union. People have a moderate view about such things nowadays. They simply ignore and when Valerie joined the staff she did the same. She felt safe with both the men. No gossips of having an affair with the boss for the privileges she got.

When she entered his room as usual there were piles and piles of papers and some pre view cassettes on his long mahogany table. HW was no fan of modern furniture. Therefore a computer and a printer looked out of place in his room. The rest of the furniture like the long chest of drawers, a big carved arm chair of the same texture, a typical English tea table in one corner with four chairs and a long floor to ceiling shelf full of books, cassettes and other ornamental pieces collected from different countries at different times, arranged in the most unfeminine style, reminded Valerie of her father's room, except her father had a smaller version.

Mr. Winslow took great pleasure in making people wait even before giving a small bit of information. He took his own time to be seated in his comfortable revolving chair and scanned through some papers out of habit rather than necessity. By the time he finished his nerve-racking gestures, Valerie had finished taking the measurements of the teak beams above, for the third time. She heard him clearing his throat, a sign for her to look at him. Without any frills he said "Valerie I want you to take a very special report."

'Well this is not unusual' Valerie thought. But she could read his eyes. They conveyed a different message today. His look was as though he was enjoying a secret excitement. May be he waited for an answer. Finding that he was not getting one he continued "Please be ready to go with the crew." well the command was given.

"But I have to finish last night's report, moreover I am not dressed..." Valerie did not finish the sentence. Mr. Winslow interrupted "Oh come on Valerie this is not the time to fish for compliments, I want this report before the others get it. It is a pretty hot stuff you know. Alen has prepared everything, you only have to read through. The camera crew is getting ready. I personally want you to do this interview because it concerns a certain lady from the high society" he raised his hand at the same time. "Well we are running short of time, hurry up and join the others." He dropped his eyes to the papers on his table and started to read one of them. Valerie knew she had been dismissed and was expected to follow orders. Shrugging she marched out without a word, knowing very well that there was no escape. One might wonder why he couldn't have left a message instead of this personal audience. Well, it was an unwritten rule in the studio that HW must personally sanction the reporter if they were not the regular ones and Valerie was actually in charge of production only occasionally appearing on screen when the situation demanded. Today was one of them.

As she entered the main hall she could see that the whole crew was busy with the preparation. Alen was already briefing the crew, and seeing Valerie, he acknowledged her with a nod, and waved some papers that he took from the scattered materials on the makeshift table. On her way to reach for the papers she stumbled once or two times on the crew sitting or half sitting on the floor taking notes. "You have exactly one hour and twenty to read the contents", Alen paused before he added "and to finish your make up." Again he turned to the crew "Ok guys, that's all. We will meet out side in…" he looked at his watch before saying "in forty five minutes." Then he followed Valerie. She glanced at the notes. There was only a short background about the situation, not many names and then there were some questions she had to ask the hotel manager about the mystery woman, When did she come? Where did she stay? Any particular room? With whom did she speak? Did he speak with her at anytime? The routine questions. She looked at the bent face of Alen. He always had a serious face which was an exception for a gay. The stereotypical squeamish movements of his type were completely absent in him. One had to observe him for a long time before even guessing that he was a gay. When she was close enough to be heard Valerie asked "Alen would you mind telling me what's going on? It will be of great help if you explain to me the subject matter," and added hesitantly "obviously you seem to be knowing that." She did not want to add 'I know you are the first to know'.

"We have information about the secret visits of a particular VIP's wife presumably connected with foreigners. It may be a hot stuff or a much ado, we have to wait and see." Just another of those cheap gossips for the 'HOT' programme. It was gaining popularity among the tabloid crowd, which liked to hear one story one day and another the next day just to entertain its shoddy taste. 'Hot' showed up to date gossips, scandals, rumours, fashions of public figures and prominent people in and around London. 'How sad that such superficial items attracted people and not more serious issues like economy, politics and environment. Well business is different from life' Valerie reflected. Sometimes one has to forget about morals if you are to survive in the world of media. They have special journalese language to attract the mass. The low morals and sordid things were referred to as trend, development, catering to the viewers taste and if everything failed they simply said marketing and profit orienting. Valerie had gone through this mill from the beginning. Now she knew how to work in the media. You appeared to be free and frank but in reality you had to sell your conscience. Nobody cared for your personal feelings. You write but it would be edited according to the day's demands. Like "We have got concrete proof" before the Iraq War and later, "We got wrong information". Valerie knew any protest on her side would only lead into losing the job. Well, if not for this occasional unpleasant interviews and third grade gossips she enjoyed the rest of her tasks. Once she was a fully fledged reporter and a consultant she could pick and chose. But till then she would be tight lipped.

Waiting outside, reading the questions and a short background of the situation, she observed the team that was accompanying her. The usual click. Alen the producer cum partner, in a grey trousers and a green pullover with the sleeves pulled up to a T shirt level, carrying a file in one hand and a box, probably with the sensitive mikes, under the other. His face was void of emotions as usual, but those shrewd eyes missed nothing. No wonder news travelled faster to the Boss, although they never saw them speaking to each other except under extreme circumstances. Whoever nicknamed him as' private and confidential', `PC´ for short, selected it not without a reason Valerie thought. Alen always took the front seat with the driver. People would think he wanted a comfortable seat but the real reason was he hated to sit with his female colleagues at the backseat.

Arranging the camera was the main camera man Mark. He knew how to make people to pose for his liking without raising his voice. At times bossy, at times arrogant. When working he made a lot of undertone comments which were not audible- he saw to that - and he had a frowning face, showing dissatisfaction with the whole world. Today he was wearing the same old red T shirt which was half tucked and half hanging showing his belly every time he lifted something. Helping him with the loading was Robert the second camera man from Harrow who came to the studio directly from his disco sessions of the previous night or to be precise early hours of the morning, without the slightest sign of fatigue. He kept the spirit of the whole team by saying some stupid things at the most awkward moment and survived with only a few grunts and rebukes. If he was allowed to work then it was because of his talent to capture people in the most unique angle. Valerie rather liked the way he said, 'Yes Miss. Wilson´ and 'No Miss Wilson'.

Carrying the mikes and the mufflers was Garry the sound man. Always perfectly dressed, smelling of G. Armani, and a man of less talk and more action. 'Garry the sound' fitted him better because he walked with sound talked with sound and most probably slept with sound. He couldn't sit still without humming or singing while working, but the funniest thing was, no one could guess the melody unless he told you. When there were pretty girls he took more time to adjust the mikes, very often changing places starting from the lapel of the coat to the bust line and lingering at the latter more than it was necessary, but he was so subtle one wondered whether he was careful with his job or otherwise. So far no complaints from the people, so he continued. As for Valerie, she got no trouble because she did it herself. But very often Valerie couldn't help putting her tongue in the cheek when he was fixing the mikes for the guests. No comment, no reaction.

Then Neil for graphics. Unlike a few years ago, when the graphics were done at the studios even for a three minute report, the new trend was to use a laptop on the spot itself to write any translation which was very often nowadays. What with so many reports about foreigners! This additional member of the crew with his laptop and CDs, and totally addicted to the computer, was more of a robot than a person. You hardly heard him talking to any one.

His bent head lifted up occasionally to have a distant look as though he was contemplating out beating Bill Gates. Any request was responded with a shrug. But as far as Valerie was concerned, Neil looked up only to breathe.

The most important member (?) of the crew was the makeup woman Röya. An Iranian by birth but British in habit, dressed in bright colours, telling everyone the British have no taste, and walking through the corridors jingling her bangles. She was quite efficient in her job and did fantastic work on people's faces. Her only weakness was that she talked too much. While doing the face her mouth would be going in every possible direction like a person with a mouthful of different chewing gums trying to taste all of them separately at the same time. What she talked about was irrelevant as long as you responded with an 'mm' to tell her you were listening. Because her command before she started the makeup was "Don't talk till I finish with you." Her talk was interesting, specially the overstress on her `r´s and a heavy accent, the absence of enunciation, wrong syllable stress, and pronouncing extra vowels added to the words with an overemphasized intonation at times. Her 'Engilish' (She means English) was good enough for her profession. 'After all make up is an art for which one must know how to use the colours with a lot of imagination and taste and it did not need any language skills' was her philosophy. And by the time she finished talking, you had the feeling you had been witnessing one of those 'Mind Your Language' episodes. (A famous series in the sixties, about a class conducted by a British teacher especially for foreigners and the fun of it.) Quite entertaining.

The last thought brought a wistful smile to Valerie's face which halted in the midway when she saw the very person walking towards her with a grin. "Hi, Miss Wilson" she never forgot to address people with respect because in Iran people did so she had explained. "Shall I start now, I think before the boys are ready I could finish with you". 'No escape' Valerie thought and nodded her head. When guests were involved Röya insisted on accompanying the crew more for the fun she would have than the real job itself.

Valerie sat on a chair facing the light and closed her eyes (mouth as well). "Well Miss. Wilson I heard this report is a hush, hush and concerns a society woman" Valerie knew Röya would continue even without her answer. So she kept quiet. Röya continued "I heard when Alen talked with the big boss" 'you eavesdropper 'was the thought in Valerie's heart but she opened her eyes to show her surprise and just as she anticipated the provocation did the trick. The torrent of words that followed gave her enough material for her report without referring to her notes. "This lady" Röya's hands stopped for a moment to show the inverted commas a typical Central European gesture meaning 'the so called', "was visiting hotels looking for foreign men" her large eyes became larger and showing detest at the same time, she continued by saying, "and the disgusting thing is her husband was also seen with her. Well I tell you, we may not have loads of money but we have better morals." She twisted her engagement ring which was the second in the past two years.

Valerie hated when someone tried to influence her before she made her own decision. Therefore she drifted into her own thoughts.' You should not create in anger what you lack in reason' she thought of the Chinese saying and tried to concentrate on how she should formulate the questions at the interview.

Once inside the van there was some kind of general discussion on the report they were going to do. All of them voiced their opinions.

"Mr. Haward is highly influential. I have often heard his name. If what we hear is true then he's really in a hot soup".

"But this is not about him. It is his wife who is involved. Maybe he is selling some secret information to the FBI through his wife" reflected Robert.

"Don't try to be a James Bond" snapped Mark.

"Although Mrs Gina Haward is a society woman, I have never seen a photograph of hers on the society column" Robert contributed.

'Once you are in the media one cannot afford to be partial. Obsessions and impressions could change in a lightening second. One wrong step could decide a place in hell or heaven. Surprises are the food for the media. Sensational head lines and apologies are common in my world. One should know the correct time to launch and to withdraw. Then you are safe'. These were the thoughts when she heard Röya's husky voice "She is not a Briton, maybe Spanish or Italian. I remember reading it somewhere", naming a tabloid, notorious for its gossip column.

There was a short break in the conversation, and at last Valerie broke the ice by saying cheerfully "Isn't it amazing that I have such a clever crew. I feel I could do the report without reading the script. Well thank you folks", and tried to relax. For the first time she regretted not reading society columns regularly. Very often names sounded familiar but not the details.

But Mark hissed "Pretty hot stuff, involving high ranking people. I hope we don't get into trouble", He rubbed his hands together briskly as if that gesture would help him to overcome his nervousness.

But Valerie cut short "Hey, hey I personally feel it is just another much ado".

"Don't take it too much for granted" Mark declared curtly, removing an imaginative speck of dust from the lapel of her suit.

****

The moment Valerie got down from the van she was aware there was an antipathy in the atmosphere. She had to try very hard to make the manager of the hotel feel comfortable. Slowly he began to come out of his shell. By the time the technical matters were fixed he was ready for the interview hiding his initial vehemence and even had the grace to smile slightly although his hands showed nervousness. Valerie was looking at the camera and waiting for the signal, to start. Alen extended his five fingers slowly bending them one by one. When the little finger bent, Valerie started the interview according to the inside –story supplied to her. "Good Morning my dear viewers. One could not say in which burrow a snake is. Well we are going to meet a faithful citizen willing to share some of the incidents which have disturbed him during the past few months." First the camera turned to focus on the street. Then it swung again to show Mr. Spencer's shadowed profile. Valerie noticed that he was a bit pale and uncertain. To put him at ease she said" Rumours don't mean much, but the truth cannot remain buried. Don't you agree? Just tell us your experience with this mysterious lady."

"Well one cannot call her a lady, may be an enchantress. I noticed her only a few months ago" his voice was nervous. His hands were fiddling with his tie while looking at the monitor all the time. There was a long awkward pause. Valerie allowed that, to give him some time to recover from the initial camera shyness, so she signalled the camera to focus the street and she got the results she expected. The fiddling stopped and he said, this time his voice more confident, "I watched this lady and I got suspicious. I asked the staff to have a careful eye on her " He became serious now. "I never allow such nonsense in my hotel." This time he looked directly at her." I was rather annoyed when I found out that they were giving fake names. ' Something fishy' my colleagues said."

"You mean to say, when foreigners came into the picture." Valerie prompted.

He nodded his head vehemently and said "I thought the whole mess will turn into a huge political brawl." Valerie pretended to be serious and raised her eyebrows. As if waiting for this, words poured out effusively from his mouth. Words like 'pretty nasty stuff', 'ensuing scandal' were accompanying his story which changed from amused contempt in to raw anger. Finding enough material for the report, Alen gave the sign and Valerie stopped the interview promising him not to show his face and to decode the voice. She thanked him in a very pleasant way that he felt exculpated.

It took more time than they anticipated. The members of the crew were having the fish and chips, talking with their mouths full and relaxing in their own way. Valerie gave an amused look at her crew. Mark was making a paper ball out of the corn shaped packing and was aiming at Robert who ducked at the nick of the time, and the paper ball fell into the cleavage of Röya's blouse. Taken aback, she spontaneously put in a hand to remove the 'invader', and cried out when her hand came in contact with the rest of the sauce. Coming to her rescue Garry tried to wipe it with his serviette and unfortunately touched her breast, a freedom on mistaken premises. A glare from Röya sent him back to where he came. Valerie the only other female member of the crew felt it was high time she intervened and went to Röya´s rescue. Alen having the last word with the manager looked at the scene with unyielding distaste. Valerie could see it was clearly agony and ill humour in his opinion. At last, with simple and general gestures of farewell they started their journey homeward. Alen was a bit pensive and the rest of the crew either tired or sleepy. When they reached the studio each busied with his or her assignment and Valerie having the permission from Alen to do her task, walked to the editing studio to finish the three minute report. As far as Valerie was concerned it was another unpleasant day, smearing her hands with other people's dirt as usual, and any ill effects were too distant to be recognised. Still she was angry with Alen and Mr. Winslow for not telling her the whole truth about the people involved and rushing her to the scene without giving her enough time to prepare herself.

Chapter 2

Valerie's father was happy when he saw his daughter. He had invited a few friends for his birthday from his school where he was the director. A party service had provided the necessary food items. It was when her father was unwrapping the birthday presents that somebody turned on the television to see the 6 o'clock news. Valerie joined the others to watch the news only half concentrating. The usual stuff in politics and then came the local news. She stood still when she heard the name Gina Haward and the photo of a very beautiful woman for Valerie could see she was definitely not an English rose but a ravishing beauty either from Italy or Spain. The reporter said "...After hearing that a television crew had mistakenly identified Mrs. Haward as the mystery woman making the nocturnal visits, Mrs Haward has taken an overdose of sleeping tablets. She was taken to the hospital in a critical condition where all the attempts to save her life failed. Mrs. Gina Haward is thirty two years old and she is the wife of the American film director Mr. Oliver Haward. Mrs. Haward comes from a highly orthodox family and could not bare the shame of even being suspected let alone accused of such a thing. She left a farewell note to her family. The contents of which are not fully revealed to the press at the time of this report. Her family which is also wealthy...", the rest of the words did not simply enter Valerie's head. Noticing the stunned look on his daughter's face Mr. Wilson asked "Is something wrong"? "Everything", she said and ran upstairs to her room and dialled her office number. No one was answering the phone. Valerie's hands were shaking and the seconds ticked like hours. She tried Mr. Winslow's number not that she expected him to be present at the office, but it was only a wish in panic. No answer. Her fingers were busy with several numbers in the hope of finding someone, whereas her brain was busy with the question 'Have they already put the trailer of the report?' At last she was able to reach the transmission room. "Hello Mark," her voice was dead flat. " Have you telecasted the trailer for tomorrow"? It sounded like a student knowing she had failed the exam, hanging on to a thread of hope. "Yes" came the prompt reply. Valerie's heart sank. Without noticing the stillness at the other end he continued. "Boss wanted to put it in the earlier edition and it went together with the Five o'clock news. We were able to show your pretty face a bit Miss. Valerie". If he expected a big thank you then he was disappointed. instead he heard " Oh no". "What's the matter"? Mark asked. "Did you see the 6 o´ clock news? It's a total disaster Mark." She did not want to waste time talking with Mark. She should either reach Mr. Winslow or his counter part Alen. So she asked "Where could I reach Mr. Winslow?". She spoke quickly with a lost battle feeling making no attempt to hide her anxiety. Sensing the urgency in her voice he said" I'm sorry he left for Dublin on the five o'clock flight to sign that deal that he very much wanted. Can I do anything"? There was an eagerness in his question." Oh please don't repeat the trailer. I will explain when I get there" "At this time"? Valerie did not reply but replaced the receiver with the same speed she took it.

What should she do now? With Mr. Winslow out of town she could only approach Alen. But where? She tried his private number. The phone was ringing. No one answered the call. 'Oh come on Alen take the receiver' she prayed. She was about to give up. Suddenly she heard the receiver being lifted and a female voice saying, "Hello" Valerie did not waste her time on introductions. "This is Valerie from the TV station speaking. May I speak to Alen please. It's urgent"

There was a small pause and a murmur before she heard another dejected voice replying" Hello this is Robert, Alen's brother. Alen has gone to the studio urgently." Now the voice was a bit clear, "May be you could try there". In her anxiety Valerie forgot her manners to say 'thank you 'but slammed the receiver. Next her fingers were busy pressing Alen's mobile number which she knew he used only when he was driving his car. " Valerie " his voice showed a tinge of nervousness or was it fear.

"Alen" she said, and before she could continue, "Valerie", his voice cut through. "I tried to call you but your line was busy. Please come to the studio now" the line went dead. Valerie ran down stairs. A few of her father's friends were lingering in the living room. She did not want to spoil his evening. Taking her hand bag and giving a big hug she said "Daddy please don't wait for me. I may be late" she was extra careful not to show what was troubling her at that moment. As for Mr. Wilson that was nothing unusual and Valerie's unearthly working hours was an accepted fact so he returned to his friends to resume the conversation.

Without further comment Valerie ran out and started her car. In her panic she took the wrong turn and seeing the mistake in the nick of the time turned her car so sharply that her breaks screeched when she headed towards the main road. She couldn't simply think straight. What should they do now? Should they apologise today? A train of questions bombarded her head. The pressure of it automatically made her foot to touch the accelerator, as though by doing it she could reduce the distance. Her mind was working faster than the speed of her car. Seeing the lights in Alen's room she went there straight away. Alen looked up with the grave face, which already showed signs of strain.

"What are we going to do?"

She shot the question without any formality

"Apology of course!" "But how? And to whom?"

"First on the TV and then to the family"

"When?"

"Now. Before it is too late."

There was a pause and then he added, "Valerie I want you to appear on the screen, that will be the appropriate thing to do", then as an after thought he added "I am sure HW won't mind. In fact I am waiting for his call at any moment. But he has a lot to answer"

Valerie nodded without knowing that this nod was determining her fate.

"Would you mind writing the script for me. I'm in no mood for that"

"Fine. You inform the recording staff. They are already at the studio.

I'll be there in fifteen minutes" he said without looking at her directly.

She left Alen's room and headed towards the studio. Signs of fatigue began to show on her face. The dark corridor scattered shadows here and there and each shadow became the dead woman. She drew herself away from the reflections and glanced with a gesture of anger. As she entered the main hall, she realised how little she knew about this lady. She cursed under her breath. She had a nibbling suspicion that Alen felt uneasy too. It was with some trepidation she entered the studio. Seconds became minutes and minutes became the next hour. There was no sign of Alen.

Valerie came out of the recording room and went to find out what was delaying Alen.

The light through the slit of the door made her to enter the room with a brief knock. She heard him pitching his voice barely above whisper and saw the astonishment on seeing her which he made no attempt to hide. A quick look on the papers on the table conveyed that he had not finished the script. On the contrary he was only talking to some one on the phone. He motioned her to sit down. And she guessed who it was more by instinct than knowledge, for Alen was saying ' Okay Harold, I will do as you told me. Valerie has just come into the room, Would you like to have a word with her?' There was a pause on this side for obviously on the other side HW was saying something in such a manner that interruption was not possible. Then she heard Alen saying "Yes... I understand... Certainly... 'he slowly laid down the receiver with a distant look in his eyes. Then he said with a frown "Harold is not in favour of an open apology. He said we could call the family and explain the matters. Since our name was not publicly announced he would prefer to leave things as they are. In case they go to the extent of filing a case, the less we say the better" he said. "I could not agree more" he spoke more to himself than to Valerie. She couldn't measure the look he gave her, and to break the tension in the air she asked "What if they decide to do so?" Alen broke his eye contact by looking at the ceiling and muttered, "Then we have to talk with our legal consultant", he was reacting like a typical calculative business man, she thought.

"We have to save the company than lingering on emotions." "So Harold and you have decided to defend yourselves."

"When it comes to that, yes."

"And what exactly is your defence?" "You will know when the time comes," was his calm reply. There was an awkward pause, as though he was reluctant to continue. Then he added, "And now you go home and sleep Valerie. Harold is taking the next flight from Dublin. We will be able to settle everything once he is here"

It triggered in her brain that Alen was hiding something from her. But she did not want to insist. She knew Alen too well. The more you pressed the more difficult he became. Without a word she left the office. Driving back she was haunted by that lovely face of Mrs. Haward. It was almost ten o'clock when she reached home. Except for the night lamp the house was in darkness. ` Well father must be sleeping. Let me not disturb him' she thought. But as she opened the door her father called "Is that you Valerie?"

Startled she said "Yes".

"What happened?"

"One of the reports that I did was not exactly the truth, and a lady has committed suicide..." she couldn't continue further. All the pent up tension came out as tears. Her father waited patiently till it subsided to whimpers. Then he heard the whole story. He broke the silence "You should have confirmed the story before you went to the spot. Why didn't you?" "Daddy when HW told me to go to the spot I had no way of protesting. And how could I know that he would make a mistake? After all he is the boss"

"What are they planning to do?"

"Alen is waiting till HW returns tonight. Of course Alen knew what they are going to do, but he did not want to tell me"

"It is too early to tell anything. But I think you have to wait and see what Harold has to say. Why don't you take a cup of black coffee which I have left in the flask and go to bed. I am sure you will be able to think clearly in the morning."

Whether she could or could not she did not want her father to sit with her the whole night which he always did when some thing happened to her, since she lost her mother at the age of sixteen.

"I will daddy, and now please go and get some sleep. The whole day you were busy and I am sure you are tired Daddy."

"Oh not for you dear." His voice betrayed his physical condition. Valerie walked with him to his room settled him comfortably in his bed and closed the door. Soon she heard his deep breathing. Satisfied with the outcome, she changed and opened the balcony door and sat down in one of the chairs. She couldn't sleep for a long time. But when she did dawn was already breaking. The morning sun woke her. She opened her eyes with confusion and numbness of the foot. Some one had covered her with a thick blanket. `Dear daddy´, she thought affectionately. But soon such pleasant thoughts were clouded with the events of the night before. Quickly she brushed, bathed and dressed and went down. Finding her father in the garden she took a step to go to him when the telephone rang. Strange enough her hands were shaking. A deep voice asked `Miss Valerie Wilson?'

"Speaking."

`You mean creature, I will never leave you in peace'

`Who are you? What do you want from me?'

`Very soon you will know. I will find you even if you go and hide yourself in hell, because that is where you will go in the end."

"Who are you? What have I done to you?"

The line went dead. She saw her father coming running from the garden." What is it dear? Who was on the phone?'

"I don't know. He threatened me for something, and I don't know for what."

Valerie's voice was hysterical. She sat down slowly in the nearby chair holding her head with her hand. Hardly five minutes passed before the telephone rang for the second time. This time she allowed it to ring for some time before she lifted the receiver. `Hello' she said weakly. "Valerie? Thank god you are at home. Harold wants you at the office as soon as possible", said Mr. Roland from the administration. Before she could ask anything further the line was dead. Weakly she got up. She answered her father's inquiring look. "They want me at the office. I better go"

Chapter 3

When she got into her car to go to the office she never thought that she would ever go there in the future. All the way to the office she was searching her mind for an answer to the stranger's accusation and not thinking about the quick summons by her boss. But when she arrived at Mr. Winslow's office she was shocked to find the current state of affairs. They all looked at her as though she was a criminal. But why?

When she opened the door of Mr. Winslow's office, two pairs of eyes turned in her direction. Silent and still Alen turned back briefly as if he was about to say something but instead became fastidious. Valerie greeted "Good morning" and to her surprise none of them returned her greeting. Without any further formalities, she looked directly at Mr. Winslow and asked "You wanted to see me Mr. Winslow?"

Mr. Winslow uncrossed his legs and leaned forward. and cleared his throat." You know Valerie, we are in great trouble." He hesitated searching for words. When Valerie was silent he continued. "This Haward business has become more serious than we first thought. Both Mr. Haward and his wife's family or rather more the latter wants to finish our company. I don't know whether you are aware that they are a powerful lot. Already they have had a word with our sponsors ".For the first time his gaze was directed at her, forcing her into accepting the fact that he really meant serious. Valerie looked at him blankly and broke the involuntary silence that invaded the room by asking, "Is there a compromise? " Neither of them spoke for a moment and both started at the same time saying "But..." and stopped as though pre rehearsed. "But what Alen", she turned her eyes in his direction. Exchanging a quick glance with Mr. Winslow he said "Unless you help us"

"How can I help?" her voice was puzzled but willing

Now Alen appealed to Winslow." Harold you better explain."

Valerie's eyes moved quickly in his direction as though she was watching a tennis match at Wimbledon.

He appeared to be seeking for the proper words and at last having decided said, "You see Valerie, the situation is like this." His voice was cold and impersonal. As if sensing what was to come Valerie frowned. Winslow continued." Instead of the company taking the blame if one single person takes the responsibility, then the legal complications are less and there is a possibility that the company could survive." Valerie did not dare to offer a comment, she simply looked at him with the expectation for him to finish the rest. So he was obliged to finish." Now comes the difficult part. Our Legal consultant said if one single person, took the responsibility we should only pay the damages or if we are lucky a public apology and that would end the matter"

"You mean you have to accept the responsibility. But that is not good for your reputation" "Of course not." He snapped under pressure and broke the eye contact. The silence that followed forced him to talk. "Either you or Alen"

For a moment she revolved in the empyrean realms of cyber space. Slowly it turned out into a quick gleam of anger "What are you trying to say Mr. Winslow? That either of us take the blame for the fault of yours? But that's not fair!" Valerie was outraged and she appealed to Alen. He was rotating the glass paper weight so earnestly as though the whole conversation was none of his concern. It was Mr. Winslow's voice that floated in the air again." In business nothing is fair. Surely you understand that as a partner of the company we couldn't afford to lose him.", his fingers pointed to Alen who was still busy with the paper weight." Moreover we need him more than..." He hesitated. Valerie felt a wave of momentary exhaustion sweep over her and she finished "...me". The silence that followed seemed to approve what she said. "But you know very well that I am not totally responsible for the report. Based on the information given by you I went. I did not initiate. I didn't have a chance to do any research on that. Then how come I take the responsibility" Valerie was breathing hard and both the men seemed to enjoy it more than sympathise with her. Instinct told her it was useless arguing. She was proved right for she heard him say "It is not about right and the wrong now. It is the survival of the company we are talking about Valerie"

"In other words I become the scapegoat", the accumulated tears at the bottom rim of her eyes was undecided whether to drop or not, but it dropped when she closed her eyes out of shear exhaustion. Tears could be a weapon or a sign of weakness. The impute brought her to inanition. This time Alen spoke. "Only two alternatives are possible. Either you take the blame and resign or we all lose our jobs" There was a numbness in her heart that made it easy to listen to him. "Valerie" he continued, "you are young and would have a lot of offers but think about all the staff who are working for so many years. They will be jobless overnight. And think about their families. They don't have a well to do father to support them." They were statements based on logic and not based on fairness. She did not see a ray of hope. She allowed him to continue." Of course Harold will give you a good reference if you resign, Won't you Harold?" as an after thought he added. Valerie looked at him with reproach.

"But on the other hand…" his voice was an octave lower now… ".if we fire you, you can't expect a reference you know."

"It is more of a moral blackmail than a kind request", she sounded flat.

"Well, take it as you please as long as you realise the decision should be made here and now". Resisting the impulse to retort, she looked at them with a blankness in her eyes. She felt as though she was looking at two selfish, overbearing, inhumane strangers. Nothing she said would be accepted until she agreed to their terms. Who would like her if they were told that she could have saved the company by stepping down so that the others could hang on to their jobs. With down cast eyes she thought ' What's the use in fighting a losing battle'. She lifted her face and stared through the window for a moment, pressed beyond the limits of human patience, she searched for the correct words and then said slowly," I hope the staff appreciates what I am going to do. But one thing," she continued," I will hate you both till I die", least realising how lame and stupid that sounded. Without any further comment she started towards the door. Half way she stopped, and added "Send the resignation letter for me to sign. The quicker I leave the better. I'll be in my room", she slammed the door hating to see the triumph on their faces.'

She was collecting her personal things and preparing to leave when she heard a knock on the door. "Come in." Alen entered with a set of papers avoiding to look directly at her and said "Valerie here are the papers you have to sign. Could you please sign them?". She nodded and grabbed the papers, but said nothing and scribbled her signature across the lines without even reading them. Then she half threw and half gave it to him. Alen gave another white cover and said "Here is your reference" she gave him a look that she reserved only for brutal infelicities of behaviour. No comment was necessary. Feeling guilty he said the only words that came to his mind. "I am sorry for..." That was the last straw for Valerie "Sorry for what Alen? Both of you planed it well ahead of my arrival. Now don't be a hypocrite. You wanted it to be like this, didn't you? What do you care about my feelings. This is what people call the crocodile tears in case you have forgotten", with these fiery words she marched out of the doors half in tears and half in deep sorrow. Her eyes were blind with tears when she walked through the corridors of the office, refusing to talk to others waiting at different corners.

Once she came out of the lift she walked towards the parking lot, opened the car door and kept the things she was carrying. She was in no mood to go home. Slowly closing the door she started to drift towards the Thames. She removed her shoes and hung them behind her shoulders and, started to walk shoving through the pebbles. She found solace in feeling the sudden prick and pain of the pebbles and sand on her naked s k i n . The hopes and dreams shattered, the stooping figure walked, lost in her own world of sadness. She sat down on a stone touching the water with her feet, unaware of the scrutiny by a man not far away. Her eyes were still closed when she felt a shadow over her face. "Excuse me" said a deep rich voice. She opened her eyes slowly and saw one shoe dangling before her eyes. Above that she looked into a pair of eyes which were dark, fathomless and cruel. Shocked by the nearness of the stranger she got up clumsily and her foot slipped, toppling her to lose her balance. A strong hand gripped her and held on till she recovered her stability. Without any introduction he asked" Are you the Cinderella who dropped this shoe? If so I am no prince." His voice was a mixture of sarcasm and annoyance. Hiding the initial shock discreetly, she said "Oh I am sorry, I must have dropped it while I was walking. Thank you" she added hastily.

"You wouldn't have cared if you have lost your shoe I suppose"

"Of course. What's the use in crying over spilled milk", she was reflecting over her present situation rather than the lost shoe. At the thought of that a hard smile appeared which did not reach her eyes. Obviously the man misinterpreted her reaction

"I understand you are made of hard stuff" he sneered. Having said that he turned and walked towards the main road. Valerie looked at the retreating tall figure. Stomach pulled in, resulting in a slight stoop, bent head, one shoulder hanging slightly lower than the other more of a habit than defect and the left hand fingers combing through the hair in a carefree gesture. Definitely he was no ordinary man. His features, dress and walk spoke for himself. But there was something familiar about the man which she couldn't quite remember. 'What the hell I am thinking when my future is at a stake' she groaned, and dismissing the stranger's image. She retraced her path back to civilisation shoving and pushing through the crowd declining the urge to break down there in the middle of the street. She had a creepy feeling that she was being watched. 'Now what is happening to me? Have I gone crazy after witnessing the horrible impasse during the past few hours'. She wanted to shout the words Dam Winslow! Dam Alen! and Dam the Stranger! But instead she muttered the words grinding her teeth as she got into her car and drove away.

Chapter 4

Watching the disappearance of the car the stranger muttered 'the fink'. There were shades of anger in different features on his face. His eyes were cold cruel and calculative, his aristocratic nose let out heavy breathing as though he was in the middle of a fight. His lower lip moved to a side and the upper teeth bit the end of the former so hard that he felt the taste of blood. On the whole he was as if in the grip of a demon. Quinn Patterchinni a man popularly known by name in the film world as the financier and the owner of several television networks in Italy, was about to do the same in Europe, and proud of his family heritage and while he was sitting in his car he vowed to destroy that arrogant, heartless minx who had dared to touch the Patterchinni realm. Every film on his blood was shouting 'an eye for an eye and a tooth for a tooth'. The frazzle of hatred and the animosity, spurting anger and moral superiority were obviously an atavistic urge rather than momentary haunt. He was in a state of moral indignation. Sitting in the car he latched his fingers behind his head, a gesture he did when he was under great pressure. Quinn Patterchinni had flown to London after hearing the tragedy of his one and the only sister Gina, the apple of his father's eye and the only female member of the Patterchinni family who could twist and turn her father to her whims and fancies. News had reached him while he was in the middle of a conference late in the afternoon, which he cancelled merely by sitting down and waving his hand. News spread in minutes and he called home and spoke very briefly with his father making sure some one was with the' senior', for he dared not use merely the name. He was airborne within the next hour. Waves of turbulence rocked and tossed him filling him with incongruous emotions. All the way he was making calls to find out what exactly happened and was informed by a reliable source about the TV channel responsible for Gina's tragedy. He was able to trace the sponsors. Maybe he was not popularly known in the United Kingdom, but he had influence with most of the companies. Things moved so quickly that by the time Mr. Winslow arrived in London, he was approached by the sponsors explaining the dangers he would face if he didn't act quickly. Quinn had a conversation with Mr. Winslow who said "I am very sorry Mr. Patterchinni, I was away on business and one of the inexperienced lady reporter had done the interview in the spur of the moment without getting prior permission from me. First thing in the morning I will dismiss her. But please spare us from a shut down." Quinn did not commit himself to anything while the hurt was still raw, and his forgiving quality was- almost nil like his father's. True he was a man of few words, arrogance laced with self confidence, stubborn, stern and heavy headed. On the whole a typical rich aristocratic Italian. His softer and weaker qualities were often disapproved by his hard core father, often referring to them as humiliating, feminine and stupid for a man of status. No wonder he wanted revenge because no one dared to cross the great Patterchinnis in Italy, and so it would be the same in any other place.

Using the situation to his advantage Quinn lost no time in obtaining the name and the private telephone number of Valerie more of a demand than a request. Mr. Winslow was more than willing to save his face at any cost. He was well aware that there was nothing in writing, and Valerie was verbally asked to do the report without any official entry. Valerie had walked into the spider's web where the story was twisted and turned in another version inter wound with sentimentality and threat. Mr. Winslow with the help of Alen, was able to show the head to the fish and the tail to the snake like an eel. And the result was some magnanimous failure in humanity itself, odd, bizarre and something sinister had happened to her.

****

Quinn wanted to supervise and make sure of Valerie's dismissal. When she came out with her personal belongings he wanted to confront her but had his second thoughts. He would have his revenge upon this woman more slowly he thought without any shame. He was puzzled when Valerie did not drive away. He thought it was a good chance to have a closer look at her so that he did not make a mistake when the time came. The dropped shoe gave him the chance he waited. He had another two hours to kill before he could get the access to the body of Gina which was to be taken back to Italy. He simply couldn't hang around without doing anything for Gina. On his way he had to pick up his Brother-in –Law, Haward at the Gatwick Airport. He would have to deal with Haward later and find out the truth about the whole affair. There were times he regretted taking him to Italy. The lesson he learned was never to mix business and family. Luckily his niece Patricia, Gina's daughter, was in Rome spending the last part of her summer holidays. Thinking of her, his anger increased. His neck muscles stiffened, and the nerves in the temple became hard and prominent with the tension.

Chapter 5

When she reached home Valerie sat on the sofa and cried bitterly to her heart's content. Of all the people why should it happen to her? How much she had trusted HW and Alen. Such blunders are usually shouldered by the Director and not by the staff. Her thoughts drifted to HW. With great reluctance she forced herself into accepting the fact that she didn't know him well. A complex character with complexes. He was a man who thought, 'Thank you' should be abolished from the dictionary, for he never said thank you to anybody. He was a man of charity only to boost his image. He was a bully in many ways although nobody said it. He often acted serpentine, not pilfered, too niggling a word. He organised the finances in such a way, even the auditors were confused how he managed showing loss but at the same time bought houses in other European countries. They were never questioned about the sources of income in some of the countries. For instance private real estate agents in Italy could buy any property with money on the one hand and deeds on the other. Such people take stacks of currencies across the boarder hidden in their cars. Whether the European Union brought the expected result for the countries concerned or not it certainly did for people like Mr. Winslow to use the hoarded money freely without facing any danger. These were the speculations circulated in the office may be exaggerated a bit, but not all. "If I am to define Mr. Winslow", Valerie thought "I would simply say a selfish man with a capital 'S'."

How very true that she was not fortunate in many things. Very often being frank had brought her more trouble than anything else. She simply didn't believe in hiding the truth even though misunderstandings were caused by them. At school and at the university friends took it for granted that Valerie would not mind owning small faults committed by them. Usually she was helpless and was unable to defend herself, and the more she tried to explain the more misunderstandings emerged.

The ictus did not kill her spirits totally. But she could not continue to stay in London. She imagined the shouting headlines that will appear on the papers the next day which might lead to her identity. It was insufferably tedious to think about the past without thinking about the future. At first she became vociferous about the injustice, slowly it subsided into a groan and an empty stare. Fortunately or unfortunately her eyes focused on the Mahogany shelf. Sally was directly looking at her from the photograph. For a moment she felt her presence, and a lightening thought struck her. Why not go to Sally, her dear sister who was her counsellor till she got married and went away to Cornwell with her husband. The idea of visiting Sally sounded the best way to flee from London, 'Not because I am a coward but I don't want these painful recollections torturing me again and again´, she consoled herself. Having resolved to do it without loss of time, she dialled Sally's number. After patiently listening to Valerie's story she suggested that Valerie should come over to her for a few days if she felt like having a break from all those commotions. Valerie did not need any further persuasion, so, she packed a few things and called a taxi, for Sally had insisted that she should not drive the whole way in this condition, instead she should take the train. Valerie called her father and told him what happened and informed about her immediate departure. Before he could say anything she bade her goodbye and got into the waiting taxi and headed towards Euston Station to catch the next train to Cornwell. She put up a bright face and tried to hide even to herself the heaviness of heart. 'It might be better, just to disappear for a while ' but her heart was full of conflicting emotions.

****

Sally got married to Trevor Frost when he was teaching at her father's school. Now he was the director of a small school in Cornwell a post he did not want to miss. Much to the misery of Valerie they moved to

Cornwell two years ago. Last year the arrival of their daughter Rosemary made their life content. Trevor always liked his Sister-in-Law Valerie, who was much younger than his wife, and treated her more like his sister than otherwise. Although the momentary mental imbalance had a lot to do with the loss of job, Valerie's decision to visit Sally was more a way of an escape than a pleasant holiday.

Euston station was packed with people seeking to go to various destinations. Wheeling her bag she managed to reach the counter to buy the tickets. "One way or return"?, the question brought Valerie back to this world. "Oh one way please" "With reservation". "Yes, please". The bank notes were exchanged for the tickets. Tucking the tickets in her purse she slowly moved to the platform. There was another half an hour for the train. Valerie bought a magazine avoiding the news papers. Valerie tried to be normal and any outsider would not even guess that she was carrying the greatest burden in her heart. The impact of a great shock is often delayed.

At last the train came and she got into it with implicit confidence. When she entered her compartment there were already a few passengers, looking at her, making no attempt to disguise their curiosity. Exchange of greetings were curt and minimal. Looking at the number, she identified her seat between a middle aged lady with her hat covering half her face, and a lethargic youngster too lazy to move his legs for Valerie to pass through. For a moment she was between his legs before she almost jumped over them, losing her balance a bit, and slumped on to her seat. The lady with the hat gave a look as though warning her to watch out for her manners. Now that she was on firm footing Valerie tried to adjust her feet, pulled the jacket that was touching the young man, luxuriously stretched and yawned. She was in a position to see the Asian couple with a little boy of six or seven sitting opposite her, who had obviously watched the whole thing and perturbed by her glance, looked away instantly to adjust their gazes in another direction. Feeling all the more than common awkwardness Valerie hid her face behind the magazine shutting off not only to the people in the train but also to the people who existed in her world, and tried to concentrate on the articles in the magazine.

She had no idea when and how long she slept but when the train jolted in one of the stations she was wide awake. The scene was different. Except for the Asian couple, her two neighbours had simply vanished. Only at the far corner more in the shadows she saw a figure presumably a man. Anger and the bitterness she had subsided exposing only fresh emptiness. Buoyed by the sense of having something to do, she smiled at the Asian woman. The woman looked quickly at her husband, intensively reading the news paper, and making sure his attention was not on her, tried to bring a kind of expression which could be mistaken as either reluctance or secret fear. Valerie did not dare to smile at her again. The compartment was almost empty. The little boy started to show some restlessness. He couldn't sit still. He was banging his foot against the seat. The father said something, obviously in their own language, without lifting his eyes from the papers he was reading. But the boy continued, the father was saying something like a chorus repeating the same thing over and over again. When the little boy saw Valerie looking at him, his speed of banging increased, enjoying every minute of it. Suddenly there was a peculiar groan from his mouth and there was an absolute halt. Valerie saw a bangled hand withdrawing quickly under the head piece of the sari. The little fellow was just looking at his thigh rubbing it as hard as he could. The father continued reading the paper, the mother looked out of the window and the boy sat there quietly trying to save his face. Valerie could not help laughing at this incident. 'Well who said men are the bosses in the Asian families 'she wondered. The deviation lifted her spirit a little. And she slowly drifted into sleep led both by physical and mental exhaustion.

****

Sally welcomed Valerie with open hands. The affection between them never died. Everything that happened in their early life was shared between them. But this `closeness ' had reduced to only affection during the past two years mainly because they were not living together any more and they seldom met. Sally a wife and later a mother in an unspoiled village and Valerie a carrier girl in the city. But the affection was never lost. So here she was enjoying the sympathy and understanding of her sister again. Especially little Rosemary was a welcomed distraction. Valerie was sure her father would be well looked after by Miss. Baker for whom her father had a soft corner. For a long time she expected a deeper attachment to develop between them. `Father needs some one other than a mere daughter' she always thought.

Though Valerie did not expect to stay more than a few days with Sally, it so happened that Trevor wanted to use this chance to attend a two weeks training in Dublin. Unable to refuse the polite request Valerie continued to stay in Cornwell and did not have the slightest chance to know the twisted version of the report and the apology that appeared on the papers, putting the whole blame on the young, inexperienced reporter and how she was forced to resign for her impertinence and the nasty piece of work. Of course names were not given to spare the embarrassment both for the company and the family concerned. Mr. Wilson saw that and he preferred to ignore by not talking to Valerie about it. What was the point in making her sadder. Sadness is better when forgotten. But he did feel sorry for his daughter.

In the media anything is sensational as long as it did not have a monotonous story. So in the days that followed new head lines like Royal weddings and scandals happening around the world simply brought the incident to an end, except for one person.

Quinn Patterchinni was determined to punish the young irresponsible creature who had brought not only shame but also irreplaceable loss to his family. He drew a beautiful plan to trap Valerie and was satisfied at the advertisement he had inserted in the news papers especially for the city edition. He was like a lion in a den waiting for the prey to walk in. To the astonishment of his personal assistant in the London office recently opened, he simply pushed the first set of applications with a note 'applications rejected'. Approbation need not be doubted.

Mr. Wilson was talking enthusiastically about Margaret (so it was Margaret and not Miss Baker) and her wonderful cooking. Valerie was sure Margaret was there smiling at him when he was praising her. Towards the end of the second week Mr. Wilson called his daughters and told that he and Margaret would like to get married. Valerie forgot what ever hell she had slipped into and congratulated them both, promising, both Sally and she would come down for the small ceremony he was having for the sake of dear Margaret. Although Mr. Wilson and Margaret had made secret arrangements some time back, they were waiting for the correct time to announce it and then Valerie's sudden departure became a cumber and they had to wait, but he did not want to delay it any longer. They anticipated Valerie's return any time of the week and finding the inevitable happening Mr. Wilson decided to break the news for both his daughters at the same time when he realised they could not postpone the matters any longer. After a quite wedding in London Mr. Wilson and Margaret went to Wales for a short honey moon. They were just returning from the honeymoon when Valerie was writing the application for the new job.

Chapter 6

The house was quiet. Sally had gone to visit one of Trevor's colleagues with Rosemary, hoping to spend the whole day with them. Her father and Margaret were sleeping late they said, the previous night. Valerie dried her hair and walked into her bed room and opened her wardrobe and scanned the dresses hanging there. Then she looked out through the window. The whether promised to be fine and sunny. She chose a floral patterned dress in white orange and yellow. Her memories were not yet cold in the grave, still she put up a brave front refusing to accept total defeat. Brushing her hair she came out and her hand reached for her hand bag and the car keys and on second thoughts, dropped the latter, resisting the impulse, climbed down the stairs, took the letter she had prepared to be posted, and started to walk the one mile distance which separated her house and the post office. She found solace in observing the easy efficiency with which she moved. The fresh morning air with the lavender smell from the near by park gave Valerie the mood to take a walk. She always loved nature and enjoyed long walks in the woods watching the animals and birds, performing the most beautiful acts, like a squirrel carrying a nut, the subtle movement of a partridge, a sparrow with a twig for its nest, and rarely a snail crossing the path. She hated disturbing them and would wait patiently till they themselves vanish, bored with their acts.

It took about fifteen minutes to reach the post office. Mrs. Moorthy the post mistress was from India, recently married to a young man from the same creed. Very efficient and pleasant. Valerie knew her for the past two years.

" Good Morning", she greeted Valerie with all smiles, adjusting her glasses, a habit she acquired when she started to wear them a few months ago. "Good Morning", Valerie replied with equal enthusiasm. She could see her husband moving at the back ground, a serious looking young man rarely smiling, and quite reserved. Mrs. Moorthy always used the first names with her customers, and chattered this and that inquiring about every member of the family. If they stayed a little longer she would even offer them a drink. Although some of them were sceptic, when she explained about the hospitality in her country, they accepted her gesture and often referred her as 'that nice lady at the post office'. Valerie got her stamp and while waiting for the change, pasted it. Before Mrs. Moorthy could speak to her further, seeing the rapid increase in the number of people behind her at the counter, Valerie bade her Good Bye' to the post mistress, came out of the building and posted the letter.

Walking back she took the main road instead of the path across the park. Her thoughts went back to her old friends and how she lost contact with them. When her father was in London Bridge, where she did her high schooling all her friends were living near by and she had a lot to do with them. But when her father was transferred to Highbury, slowly she lost contact with many of them. Then in college education she had new friends. But due to different careers they drifted apart and got globally distributed, and Valerie consoled herself having friends at the working place. Her thoughts flew back to her colleagues. None of them called her, may be they had, in her absence, but when she thought about them she could not say whether she had to treat them as friends or acquaintances. After all they were people whom she knew after she joined the staff. You could not expect anything from mere acquaintances. She was unceremoniously down sized and no one came to console her. Not even a letter. When there is prosperity you have friends and when adversaries come they vanish into thin air. That is life.

"Thank god" she thought "I am not disappointed, it only hurts, but" she reflected philosophically, "one should not judge people by ones own standard". She was intimidated by an uneasy muddle feeling. The mysterious oasis we crave for is often like bubble, shinny and colourful one minute, flat and empty the next. Some sort of real truth was communicated and shared within her, till a driver tooted his horn for her to realise that she was walking on the middle of the road. Raising her hand to say sorry for the driver, she paused under the elm tree and pulled herself to the present. She pondered over the application just posted. A wink of hope perhaps. This month had gone only in dreams. Bad mostly. Perhaps this application might bring the load off her mind. But the requirements were so specific as though they already knew the candidate. That was often the case nowadays. Perhaps they have already chosen the candidate, but inserted the advertisement for the sake of formality. For a minute she wilted and her steps faulted, her hand flicked nervously towards her mouth, but she waved, away the doubts as absurd and groundless. In the radiance of these revelations, she reread the advertisement slowly.

> *A popular Television net work in Europe requires the services of an unattached lady, with some experience, between the age of 24 to 28 to work in their Berlin branch office started recently. The candidate will be a production cum marketing assistant for the beginning. Along with professional qualifications she must have a pleasing personality. It is essential that she holds a British passport which could be used at any moment. Please attach a recent photograph. The selected candidate will be called for a personal interview if needed. Good prospects. Salary and other details will be discussed in person.*

There was no name of the company, only the Post Box number in London. Luckily there was no mention about reference. Well the wind was blowing on her side. If she was selected, it would be incredibly good for her ego. Of course her reference letter said' Miss. Wilson is leaving on her own accord'. One lie would lead into the other. It was better she told the truth when the time came. The thought was more of a habit rather than a discipline for her. Valerie felt as though some one had passed her a warm coat and put its arms round her shoulder. She had equanimity beyond, her wildest dreams. Gone are the deep sighs of despairs and the staring into distance. Dispelling her own delusions about expectations from friends for understanding, sincerity and other standards of morals, she prepared herself accepting the fact that people fuss, whine, manipulate, gossip and call you vile names when occasion demanded. She remembered reading somewhere "life is ten percent what happens to you and ninety percent how you react to it ".Valerie felt she had changed. For better or worse she should wait and see. The only thought that lingered was "Will I get this job?"

****

"You are going to get this job" Quinn Patterchinni uttered the words with hatred, looking at Valerie's photograph ' It had taken me more than a month and five repeated ads to reach you, and now that I have you I am not going to let you go ' he thought with stormy intensity and maddening rage. He had purposely delayed an answer to look natural. But when he asked Jessica not to repeat the advertisement, she knew he had taken a decision. He rose from his Swedish console table tilting the coffee cup and pushed the Luis XVI style chair and walked along the matching Swedish side table with the white orchid against the ivory coloured wall. He had only one single application in one hand with his carefully planned reply written and the rest of the applications on the other. Instead of calling in the intercom he personally took it to Jessica Johnson, his personal assistant at the London office. "Miss Johnson" he said with a peculiar expression "Please type this letter of appointment to this lady," he named an exorbitant salary that it took some time for Miss Johnson's mouth to close in a slow motion. Quinn looked straight into her eyes and said "If every thing works out well, make arrangements for her to leave London in a fortnight." He turned to go and as an after thought said "I have a lot of paper work to catch up, so be quick," he paused before he added, "and I am going back to my hotel. You know where to find me if I am needed." Jessica's feminine instinct warned her ' the calmer the man is the deeper his thoughts are'. For some mysterious reason she felt this powerful man was under a strain. Walking back to his room Quinn did feel the strain or was it relief?

While typing the reply, Jessica was quite astonished the way Mr. Patterchinni (for no one dared to speak to him using the first name, an unwritten law in the office) was selecting a person to work in his new office. Usually he put them through the mill before he finally agreed. She remembered attending two interviews before being selected. And even that Quinn himself was present. But this... "Well this is nun of my business" she reflected and started to type the letter quickly. The urgency Quinn showed on this appointment was hot foot, so she better do it as quickly as possible. "Dear Miss Wilson... Sincerely yours," the printer was finishing the last sentence of the letter. If she took it now she would be able to get Quinn's signature before he left. To her surprise she saw Quinn half sitting on his table, one leg touching firmly to the ground, the other swinging, and tapping his fingers of one hand to the other, as though he was waiting only for her entry.

"I am taking your fate in my hands. No one, I say no one is going to change it what so ever" the maddening self assured spirit prevailed and his Italian aristocratic blood never accepted defeat. Who could stand the wrath of a volcano or the tidal wave once it had started. Vanity is a weakness. It would require something more radical to revitalize the spirit. Perhaps losing two important women in his life was reason enough to revenge the same. With a grim face he put his signature, as though he was signing a death warrant. Before he left the office he took out the photograph of Valerie and looked hard at her, absorbed in the past. The turmoil flooded from his heart to his eyes and the intensity of his stare was so cruel for a moment he thought the face in the photo cringed. Satisfied with the effect he walked out of the office only waving a goodbye to Jessica and nodding to the other members of the staff in the outer office. For Jessica, relief flooded in every cell of her body when he left. If her boss was in the office she was always in tension. She took care not to displease him in any way. At the age of fifty a job like this was a dream. Talking with Hollywood personals and having a fat pay with all the other comforts were things she did not want to lose. Giving a quick glance before closing the door, she returned to the constant mechanical roaring and buzzing world of work.

Chapter 7

One week had passed since she sent the application and slowly losing hope Valerie was occupied with Sally and Rosemary who continued to stay for some more days. Rosemary was just starting to walk and she was attracted by any colourful object. The house had long lost the habit of having walking babies so every time she went quickly, Valerie had to go quicker to remove the object and keep it out of reach. Sally took the opportunity to do some shopping and visiting her old friends. Mr. Wilson and Margaret took chances to give all the indulgence and petting for Rosemary, that the discipline Rosemary learned living with mamma had been forgotten, and when Sally came after her enjoyable shopping sprees she was too tired to observe them. But that day she came early and tried to give her a wash and then started the tantrums of Rosemary. She refused to leave the toys, and when removed fell on the floor throwing her legs and arms in different directions and gave such a scream that Valerie browsing some documents in the next room rushed there, thinking something terrible had happened. The exhaustion after the long day made Sally lose her temper. She accused Valerie of not knowing the limits as far as Rosemary was concerned, adding "If this goes on, soon Rosemary will go out of hand. I think the earlier I go the better ". Although Valerie knew the words were uttered in shear frustration, it hurt her to such an extent she simply walked out of the room without a word. Very recently she had become very sensitive and tears rolled down for the slightest reason. It took more than half an hour for Rosemary's cries to subside and by the time Sally managed to put her to bed she felt her whole energy was used up.

She came down and sat on the sofa facing her sister. She knew she was in the wrong, but pride prevented her to even the matters between herself and Valerie. As for Valerie, negativity came flooding back. She poked and prodded, fingered, plucked and pried into the documents she was having in the hand. Even this stopped after a while. There was a profound silence where even angels feared to tread. Valerie felt the presence of Miss Everet, her English teacher in the fourth grade, reading the poem with the intonation that of the poet himself.

> *"Some one came knocking at my wee small door,*
> *Someone came knocking I am sure,- sure –sure,*
> *I listened, I opened, I looked to left and right,*
> *But naught there was a stirring, in the still dark night"*

It was so eerie and frightening when those lines were read in the class, and the same shiver went through her body now. This egocentric Sally was new to her.

None of them wanted to break the ice at first. Then spilling all the guilty thoughts and secrets into the stomach, Valerie asked "Sally is something wrong?" Her little sister's concern made Sally feel even more guilty. She said "Oh perhaps I was torn between the free time I enjoy here and the monotonous life I would have in Cornwell." Her voice was void of feeling. Valerie was taken aback by this reply.

"What do you mean?"

"Well sometimes the loneliness kills me. I think of the days I lived here wishing to have more than twenty four hours a day to chill and chat, But now I firmly believe twenty hours are more than enough for a day. You know what I mean?" her eyes appealed fervently to Valerie. Seeking for proper words, Valerie asked "What is digging you?"

With inanition she replied "I am pregnant."

Valerie couldn't help saying "Oh that's won..." then seeing Sally's expression, her voice stopped half way in the mid air.

"It is not, at least not for another year or two. I simply can't manage alone. But Trevor wants the baby he says it is easy to bring up two rather than one"

"Then you could come here for the delivery. I and Margaret are here", Valerie uttered the words.

Sally shook her head "That would not work out, Trevor hates to be left alone too long. Yesterday when he called he sounded a bit dejected. Not that he said any thing directly, but I know. I am thinking of taking the afternoon train tomorrow." She paused to catch her breath which was but natural in the seventh week of pregnancy.

Silent and still Valerie's lips parted briefly as if she was about to say something. Sally waved away and said, "Oh forget it." Valerie thrust around for a way to pull the conversation back together. But from the tight lip and the distant look of Sally, she knew the mood of intimacy had gone.

The news of Sally's departure was received with mixed feelings by Mr. Wilson and Margaret. Well decisions made by an adult were never questioned. And Valerie decided to keep Sally's confession to her self.

The next day, preparations finished for the journey Sally brought down Rosemary, now comfortably sitting on mamma's hip. She was in a good mood after the sleep, and smiled brightly. Her slightest smile was enough to call down the angels. With hugs and kisses and waving till the figures disappeared, Sally and Rosemary were taken to the station by Valerie. Both of them did not want to open the subject of the previous evening.

The journey to Euston was short and the whole time Rosemary was trying to say a few new words unsuccessfully and was helped by mamma, and Valerie pretended to enjoy as though last night's exchanges never existed.

Back in her brain Valerie heard "Life is a stage and we all are actors, carrying the mistakes, failures, sadness and disappointments, happiness, enjoyments, success, humour, desires, hopes and life it self, showing them when we feel and hiding them when we need, with raised curtains that never come down to say the play has ended only the scene ends when new actors come and the old ones vanish" A passage read at the drama school year after year as a routine, made some sense now.

Chapter 8

Valerie was not there when the post arrived. she had gone to do the weekly shopping at the local departmental store, a habit she developed after Margaret came to live permanently in their house as her step mother. Usually Mr. Wilson's friends dropped in during the week ends knowing very well Mr. Wilson can set a fire in the river. Parents, teachers and friends with gloomy faces troubled looks and down cast eyes rarely left without a transformation. In other words their house during the weekends was more crowded than week days. But this weekend Mr. Wilson had invited the sectional heads of the school to have a business cum pleasure meal. As a weekend special Valerie and Margaret sat and planned a meal and decided to have Special chicken broth with puny lentils, tender carrot salad with prawns and coconut dressing with olives and bruschetta. The dessert was Mascarpone cheese cake with apricot and amaretto.

Margaret started the preparation and her hands were full when Valerie left the house promising to come as quickly as possible with the sherry and liquor needed for the evening.

The back seat of the car was packed with things when she stopped at the bakery to purchase some pastries that she wanted to serve with the typical English tea earlier in the evening. Entering the bakery and surveying the offers in the glass cupboards she smelt the strong aroma of the coffee brewed by Mrs. Armstrong. The temptation was so high she stopped toying with the idea and simply ordered one cup and sat down at the corner table close to the window. Mrs. Armstrong came hurrying with the coffee and seeing no waiting customers, parked her self on a bigger chair standing against the wall. A plump lady in her sixties with large bosoms and a big back. The chain watch that hung round her neck settled cosily on her bosom giving her the least trouble to see the time. Flesh was hanging from all parts of her body. Her legs were criss-crossed with varicose veins and one could rarely see the wrinkled skin in between them. Although she was diagnosed to be Diabetic she never stopped eating cakes. Her heart was pure, innocent and warm. Valerie smiled at this plump affectionate woman and asked" How do you do Mrs. Armstrong?"

"A little tired, but in the best cf spirits.", she said.

"Doesn't Arthur help you in the bakery"? Her face was passive as though those ears heard only what they chose to hear. Valerie gave up and stopped asking anymore questions. Then suddenly she said "Oh the poor man has gone to Wales for the weekend." But her eyes were staring out through the window as though astonished. Valerie followed her eyes and saw two magpies on the windowsill. Mistaking Mrs. Armstrong's reaction she frowned.

Then the old woman said "You know dear, these two birds very seldom sit on my windowsill. If they do, they bring good luck to the persons who saw them. I think you and I are lucky today."

Valerie did not want to diminish that happiness by adding any rude remark about her believes, so she only said "How nice". Then looking at the time she got up and chose her pastries while Mrs. Armstrong limped to the counter. Leaving the bakery she walked towards the car secretly wishing for that luck!!

****

Margaret looked through the window when Valerie's car entered the house. She always treated Valerie as her daughter even before she married Mr. Wilson. As a fan of Jane Austin she always compared Sally to Jane and Valerie to Elisabeth, not because of their appearances but because of their temperaments. The simple Sally accepting the life and the vibrant Valerie fighting for the rights. After all she had been close to the family for the past ten years after her dear friend Faith, the girl's mother died. The association with the family was so long that moving into the house was not a big strain or anxiety, but simply from a holiday home to the haven itself. Death comes to a family to forget the past regrets and to look forward to the future hopes. Why do people say time heals. Because once the shock is over and the hopelessness surfaces, the logical thinking hit at the back and pushes you forwards. It is only the first step that you need then you go forwards. No reverse. And the second lap starts. It is an apriority connected with the word 'fate' for the cowards and weaklings, and 'wisdom' for the brave and strong.

****

Valerie closed the front door and carried the parcels into the kitchen. Margaret remembered the official looking letter that arrived soon after Valerie's departure. Thinking it may be of importance she said "Valerie dear there is a letter for you by the morning post. I kept it on the dining table. Go and have a look at it." she cautioned her step daughter. Wondering who has written the letter Valerie neared the table. The address was typed to Miss. Valerie Wilson. She looked at the official stamp 'QP Enterprise' in golden embossed print. Looked pretty expensive. For a moment she went blank and then slowly recovering, she opened the cover hastily with shaking hands and unfolded the expensive paper.

"*Dear Miss Wilson,*" it began, 'another rejection perhaps' her heart sank. Her eyes made a quick scan through the contents.

With great pleasure we inform you that you have been selected for the job advertised on last month's news papers for a production assistant. We will be glad if you could report at our office with your original documents for a personal interview at your earliest, to discuss the details. Please make sure that your passport and other documents are up to date as you may have to leave London shortly. Your salary particulars and the agreement are attached here with. Either call in person or give a call to confirm your consent to make the necessary arrangements. Any questions or clarifications could be done with my secretary Miss. Jessica Johnson.

I hope you will have a pleasant time working in our company.

Sincerely yours,
Quinn Patterchinni
Managing Director.

'It can't be true', she uttered half croaking. The name sounded familiar, but she could not place it. A peculiar notice came out of her mouth which could be mistaken for a great shock or a great surprise. Margaret stopped stirring the soup for a moment and asked " Is anything that matters " she sounded alarmed. But Valerie burst into laughter, with tears running from her eyes at the same time. Her voice was cackled with excitement when she said "On the contrary, its good news. I have got a new job. I can't really believe that it is happening", she finished between sobs and laughter.

Soon the explanations and the commotion ended and Valerie concentrated on doing some thing practical. First thing on Monday, she called QP Enterprises and asked for Miss Johnson.

"Hello Jessica Johnson speaking" answered a very friendly voice. "Oh hello! This is Valerie Wilson speaking"

"Oh hello Miss Wilson! I hope you received our letter"

"Yes, of course, Thank you. In fact I called to say that I would accept your offer"

There was a short pause at the other end. 'Perhaps they are having second thoughts' thought Valerie. When she heard Jessica's voice again she understood that she had only changed the telephone while the voice she heard now was clear of all disturbances in a normal office. "Excuse me I had to take my personal phone so that I could talk to you without the noise of the printer. Well dear, so you have decided to accept our offer. That's good. I am sure Mr Patterchinni will be glad to hear that. He was well pleased with your application. The interview is only a formality.

Would it be possible for you to drop in at our office tomorrow morning, since I see you don't live so far from our place.

"Yes, of course Miss Johnson. Would 10 O'clock be alright?"

"That suits me. By the way Miss Wilson bring your passport along with the other documents. We may have to book the passage for you to Berlin". What luck to get a job without much formalities Valerie beamed with happiness.

"That I will do. One question Miss Johnson" "Yes" there was impatience in her voice.

"As you mentioned Berlin, I have to warn you that my German is not so perfect", Valerie did not want them to be disappointed.

"That was not particularly required. So don't worry. Mr Patterchinni knows what he wants from his employees."

"Yes I understand", which she did not.

"So, till tomorrow. Good day Miss Wilson." The dismissal was clear. "Good day Miss Johnson"

Valerie slowly replaced the receiver. "Well, that is over for the moment", but she could not stop wondering about this Mr Patterchinni. `What sort of boss was he to appoint a person without even seeing her. Well after all it is his problem´, she dismissed the suspicion.

The next day dawned with perfect sunshine. Valerie chose to wear her apricot dress. It had a simple cut, especially emphasising her perfect figure in a very special way. She wore her mother's pearl ear drops with a bear neck showing the marvellous skin in contrast to the colour of the dress. Her hair was tied at the back in a sophisticated fashion. She did not want to look overdressed. Valerie usually wore little makeup and today was no exception. A touch of transparent gloss lipstick was the only striking part on her, but it displayed her sensitive mouth in a provocative way.

Jessica was quite impressed with the person who was standing before her.

"I am sorry you can't meet Mr Patterchinni today. Though he is in London he had other important things to do before he leaves to Berlin.

Perhaps both of you will be travelling together or you will meet him in Berlin, Miss Wilson". Jessica was talking while checking the passport. There was a kind of disappointment in Valerie's heart which she quickly hid with a perfect smile.

This girl is definitely a smasher, and a threat to Quinn's bachelorhood´, Jessica couldn't help thinking. A frown appeared on her face. Valerie misinterpreted it and said "I am sure I understand that."

"And now we will go through the formalities" said Jessica ignoring her comment.

The next hour was spent on checking all the details that were needed. At last it was decided that she would leave for Berlin in ten days time. Before confirming the date Jessica called Quinn. Watching the conversation between them, Valerie noticed surprise spread over on Jessica's face after she said "You will never believe, that the original is astonishing" for Valerie heard her saying "No wonder". Placing the receiver she looked at Valerie and asked, "Have you ever met Mr Patterchinni, Miss Wilson?"

Valerie was confused for a moment and then collecting herself said "Eh...not to my knowledge, Why do you ask Miss Johnson?"

"Oh nothing, I just thought"

When Valerie came out of QP Enterprises with the letter of appointment in hand she was simply floating in the air. She was humming the song 'I could have danced'. The delay for the lift was pleasant, the cigarette smell did not irritate her, the stares and glances of the people were charming and even the dustbin looked beautiful. How very strange that when people enter the first step of joy they voluntarily enter into their own crazy utopianism. After all only the wisest and the stupidest never change and she was neither. She had a strange feeling that she was being watched by someone. Instinctively, her eyes turned up to the windows of the building. There was no one. "Don't be silly you stupid thing, who cares what happens to you", she said to herself. Opening her car door she noticed a BMW turning round the corner and disappearing. Other than that there was nothing remarkable around the place. She got into her car and drove away.

Quinn was having a tea break between his consulting sessions at the Intercontinental when he received Jessica's call. He couldn't continue with his tea, so he excused himself for half an hour and went for a drive in his car. `I only want a break' he told himself. But he automatically drove to his London office and parked the car slightly away from the building. Lighting a cigarette he sat in his car. Ten minutes passed. What was he waiting for? He did not have the answer. At that time Valerie came out of the building and walked towards her car. Quinn slowly started the engine and headed towards the hotel. `What are you trying to do, hiding yourself like this and running like a coward?' he asked himself. `What harm if I make sure she is the person whom I really want. Now everything is in place. In ten days time my sweet revenge will start and then I will be happy. For more than a month I have spent sleepless nights because of this irresponsible woman. It's high time she paid the price', his handsome face showed a touch of sadness. He thought of Patricia. His heart softened. The last time he saw her she asked "Uncle Quinn why did Mummy go to heaven?" and he could only answer "Because of a stupid devil. I can't bring Mummy back dear, but I can ruin the devil when I get hold of her". When he said this his heart bled for the little girl.

Chapter 9

"By the time you go to Berlin it will be autumn, with wind and rain" said Margaret to her step daughter affectionately. "So you'd better take some warm clothes with you". Valerie looked up from what she was doing and said, "You are right Margaret. I don't know what I would have done without you. Do you think I should take my own clothes or should I buy some new ones in Berlin to suit the office in which I am going to work"? "Well, both dear", replied Margaret. Valerie really thought that the minimum luggage she took the better, but she did not want to contradict Margaret who insisted she took the maximum. That was the trouble with her, she hated to make people unhappy if she really liked them. And Margaret was a darling with a soft heart. It was hardly two days more for her journey to Berlin and still she was not sure what to take and what not to.

Only that morning Miss Johnson called and said that she would be met by one Miss Klein at Tegel Airport. She was the public relations officer for the Berlin office. A furnished flat would be at her disposal and weekly help would arrive to do the chores. For the first few days she would be picked up by Miss Klein who would take her to the office. Once she got used to the travelling she would get her own vehicle. She was asked kindly to collect all her papers and tickets the next morning.

Valerie sat down to have a cup of coffee. During the past week she had thought a lot about her future boss, Mr. Patterchinni. Somehow or the other she could not imagine him as a young person and from what information she got from the internet she knew about the fifteen years history of the firm, its roots in Italy, a branch set in London a few years ago, and the recent addition of the Berlin branch, and a lot about the achievements in the past and its connection to the Hollywood, about which she was a bit surprised. But nothing more than the name and the qualification of Mr. Quinn Patterchinni the director of the firm. Although Miss. Johnson was lavish with various other details, she was tight lipped regarding any information about her boss. Naturally Valerie found it embarrassing to ask any kind of information about his personal appearance. So what?, she tilted her head in a peculiar way when she did not want to accept defeat, "Sometime or the other I am going to meet him, so why the hurry?"

The day before her flight she went to QP Enterprises to collect the envelope containing all the necessary documents and her tickets. Miss Johnson was called away on urgent business but had left the envelope together with another cover containing the advance on her salary partly in Euros and partly in travellers' cheques. Miss Johnson's assistant apologised for her absence and handed over the covers to Valerie and wished her a happy journey. Getting out of the lift she collided with a man. She quickly recovered realising that it was her fault and looked up into a face that was slightly familiar, shockingly handsome and definitely not English. Speechless for a moment she stared at him. But the look he gave shook her with fear and she said "Oh, I am sorry".

"Are you really?" 'How rude he is', she thought. But some how he sounded familiar. Had she met him before? The lift door closed halting her contemplation and she turned towards the entrance. Outside the sun was shining and Valerie tried to ignore the man thinking `may be he just got the sack from his job'. She giggled to herself as she got into her car. She had a few other errands to finish before she left, so she focused on them forgetting the whole incident.

Back in the office, Quinn simply could not concentrate on his work `This girl always upsets me. The more I see her the more I hate her. I should do something quickly' he vowed to himself. He called the Berlin office and informed them his date of arrival.

****

Though Valerie hated farewells and last minute emotional exchanges she couldn't refuse when her father and Margaret offered to drive her to the airport. She was taking the Friday morning flight so that she could have time to rest and get acquainted with Berlin, before she started to work on Monday. Due to the rush of the weekend crowd she could not wait for a long time in the lounge with Margaret and her father. By the time Margaret kissed her with that maternal instinct and her father wished her the best, Valerie heard her flight being announced. Taking her hand baggage she started to enter the restricted area with the name `Passengers Only'. "Here I go on my new venture" she told herself as she found her seat in the plane. She took out a magazine and started to read. Then remembering that the time in Berlin would be an hour ahead she adjusted her wrist watch. `Two hours straight flight' they said. What was in store for her? a little fear cropped up.

"Fasten you seat belts, Please". `No turning back' Valerie smiled.

Chapter 10

Valerie must have gone to sleep because she was awakened by the announcement "Fasten your seat belt please. We will be landing the Tegel Airport of Berlin in ten minutes." Valerie opened her hand bag and took out a small brush and brushed her hair, redid her lip and looked into the mirror. Her outfit was standard and the lemon colour suited her dark hair. After the formation of the European Union a few years ago, the checking for British passengers at the Berlin airport was almost nothing. Valerie was allowed to go as soon as she identified her luggage. Pushing it in a trolley she came out of the customs. When she walked out a few heads turned in her direction, for nobody could resist that kind of beauty. She was one of the few dark heads among the blondes.

She heard a very sweet voice calling her name. She turned in that direction," Miss Wilson I am here on your left". She looked at the owner of the voice. A smartly dressed blonde was waving her hand to her. She had a bunch of flowers on one hand and a stuffed pig on the other. She met her halfway and introduced herself. "I am Susana Klein from the QP Enterprises. Welcome to Berlin." handing over the bunch of flowers and the pig she said, "Pigs are our good luck charm you know"

„Oh thank you very much! it's lovely! and thank you very much for meeting me". Valerie said, then she asked her "How did you identify me"?

"Well the London office sent an e- mail with your photo. Even otherwise you could be identified", she said with a meaningful glance.

"You look charming Frau Klein", Valerie added hesitantly.

Valerie knew that German ladies preferred to be called 'Mrs' rather than 'Miss' which is used exclusively for teenagers. The word 'Frau' is a neutral word for both married and unmarried ladies. She knew the amount of formalities the Germans observed, the so called ' German bureaucracy. Interrupting her thoughts Susana said "Oh call me Susana, when you call Frau it adds to your age you see." A slight dimple appeared on her face which Valerie found very attractive. 'I must remember that in future' Valerie mused. Susana continued "Are you hungry or would you rather go to your flat and have a bath?"

„Do we have to go out for the meal?"

"Well today yes. But tomorrow you can make your own arrangements"

"In that case I will have the meal before we go to the flat. Because I would like to have a long bath"

"I understand", Susana said with a smile.

They entered the Airport restaurant with the self-service system. Valerie chose a salad and an open sandwich with cheese. Susana only drank a glass of apple juice and helped Valerie to carry her glass of orange Juice.

Travelling from the airport to her new flat Valerie studied the new place where she would be working in the future. The streets were clean and the buildings were well maintained. She saw some beautiful parks with inviting looks. But, she was mostly attracted by the tons and tons of roses grown along the streets. "What a beautiful place Berlin is", she whispered aloud. Susana who was concentrating on taking a very sharp curve said, "But you won't say that when you see the East side of it. It is a pity it had been neglected for many years, though the government is taking every measures to compensate that" She sounded a bit sad.

"Forgive me if I am rude. Are you from the West side or form the East?" Valerie asked and spotted a shadow passing over Susanna's face before she answered.

"Well I am from the East, but now there is no such difference though".

Valerie felt as though she had invaded into the limited territory, and felt a sort of passive resistance. She was about to apologise for her question, but then she heard Susana's clear voice "Otherwise I wouldn't have got this job, you see. But it will take a long time for us to forget the past. Luckily I grew up with my parents. But there are children who saw either of them only after twenty five years". Encouraged by her openness Valerie asked

"Do you really believe this feeling will continue?"

"Can't say."

Some sort of real friendship was shared between them. Valerie understood that Susana would rather not talk about it further, so she changed the subject. "I heard the Berlin office is rather new. How many of you work here"? "Though it is new, there are about twenty permanent staff and another thirty on contract basis. I heard very soon it will be the main office in Europe. The boss intends to extend the firm not only for television but also for big film projects. Any way Berlin is better than Rome and cheaper than London."

There was a long awkward pause when Valerie did not answer.

"What made you to take this job, so far away from your home?" Now Valerie had to answer.

"Well challenges make you discover things about yourself that you never really know"

"Great souls have will whereas weak ones only have wishes" reflected Susana looking at Valerie with admiration," Brains and beauty is a rare combination"

Valerie knew that was a 'no comment' statement. So she ignored and pretended to look out of the window. They were just passing a tower and then a very impressive huge comparatively long building in the form of a ship.

"What is this building?" Valerie showed an interest.

"Oh the tower is the Radio Tower and the building is the International Congress Centrum." "Quite attractive "

"Wait till you see some beautiful architecture in the East Berlin"

Valerie acknowledged with a smile. Then she asked "Where did you learn your English Susana"?

"Oh we were not taught in the school. We were taught Russian you know. But soon after the reunification I went to a special English School and learned English. I passed the Trinity college examinations and did a one year course in Effective Communication. Now most of the firms ask English for any job", she smiled.

Before Valerie could speak again Susana said, "Here we are. Your flat is in the first floor. They haven't put your name yet, but on Monday every thing will be there. I will come with you and show you the flat, and then I have to rush to the office to do some more errands and in the evening I will collect you for dinner."

"Quite a tight schedule" Valerie echoed politely.

Susana helped Valerie with her baggage, walked to the front of the building, took out a bunch of keys and separated one bunch from the others. She inserted the key with mathematical precision and opened the big door. Keeping her foot to the door she dragged one of the bags and put it near the hinge preventing the door from closing. Then she swung the other bag swiftly and efficiently. Valerie could only watch with surprise. "How could you do that?" she couldn't help asking. "All the military training in the DDR" she replied half jokingly.

Some people were just coming out of the lift and Susana was quick enough to halt the door from closing. Valerie just pushed one bag in its wheel with her foot and took the second in her hand. Standing comfortably between the bags the two of them reached the first floor. Valerie was busy taking the baggage out of the lift, and seeing she could manage, Susanna took the bunch of keys again and selected another one to open the door of the flat. Then she came and helped Valerie to carry the bags `Phew" said Susana closing the door. Valerie measured the flat. "Before I forget Miss. Wilson, be careful with the keys. Here in Berlin, if you loose the key it will take some time to get another set. By that time, the bad guys would have robbed your flat". "Don't scare me Susana. By the way you can call me Valerie if you like. And that is when you want me to call you Susana. I feel old when you put the 'Miss '. Both of them laughed heartily. "Done" said Susana with her thumb up, a gesture Valerie had to learn in the coming days. After showing the flat and the whereabouts Susana showed the food that was stocked both in the refrigerator and in the store room. Having done everything that was needed Susana said "Good. Now listen, tonight I will come and pick you at Eight O' clock. I know a very good Italian restaurant near your place. This is not official you see. Only both of us"

"That's fantastic. At what time should I be ready Susana"?

"Well I will call you at about seven. Will it be alright"?

"Suits me and Thank you, Susana".

Susana gave the telephone numbers she could be available twenty four hours. When she left the flat she was all in smiles that Valerie felt at least she had one friend in Berlin. Out of habit she said "Tschüss" in German and Valerie returned the same politely.

Valerie put the flowers in a vase and started to unpack her things. When she sat on the sofa she remembered that she had not called her father and Margaret. She took the number and remembered to add the country code. She heard her father's voice at the other end:

"Valerie dear how nice to hear from you. How was the journey?"

"It was quite nice. Berlin is beautiful daddy I think I will be happy here."

"Good to hear that. What ever happens don't loose hope. Daddy is always here"

"Thank you daddy. Could I say hello to Margaret Daddy"

"Unfortunately not. She was called for an urgent counselling at the local centre. But I am sure she will call you soon."

"Covey my love. Oh! before I forget here is my private number and when I go to the office on Monday I will be able to give you my office number too. Till then, Daddy", She gave the telephone number before she replaced the receiver.

Chapter 11

Valerie was looking like a picture when she finished dressing for the evening. She was wearing an off shoulder dress in deep blue. A small ear stud glittered on her ears. The French twist of her hair displayed the long slender neck of hers very distinctly. She found a pair of high heeled shoes to match the dress. Thinking the weather might be cooler later in the night she took a light coat in the hand. She was checking for the keys and money in her hand bag when the door bell rang from out side. Pressing the intercom she asked "Susana?"

"Yes", Susana replied," Valerie would you mind coming down. I will wait in the car right in front of your door step. There is no parking place close at hand." "And Valerie", she added, "don't forget your keys"

"Sure, give me a few minutes to close the Windows" Valerie pressed the button to cut the intercom.

When she came down and got into the car Susana gasped and said" I am sure a few men will be following us when we return." Valerie looked at her companion with a frown. "Because I myself feel like falling in love with you!" she exclaimed.

"The feeling is mutual" said Valerie admiringly looking at the blonde girl. Susana giggled and started the car. They were driving through a very colourful road and Valerie asked "Which part of Berlin are we now?"

"This is the famous Ku'Damm area which is the centre of the city, although Potsdammer Platz is gaining popularity in the recent years."

"Isn't this area famous for night life if I am not mistaken"

"Correct. Don't try to walk alone in the nights in this area. It is not safe if you are not familiar with the place. You will run into trouble", she said with a meaningful laugh.

"I understand. I will be careful. Susana"

The drive did not take even ten minutes, before Susana was looking for a parking place." We are going to Restaurant Olive, small but excellent food. "Typical Italian", she said offing the engine. "I would love it" said Valerie getting out of the car. Susana locked the car and led her to a beautiful restaurant. They were welcomed by a lady whom Susana said as the wife of the' owner. Selecting a corner table Susana settled in the place after removing the coat and giving it to the hostess. Valerie followed suit. Valerie did not want to have anything strong so she ordered for a glass of dry white wine, while Susana had a glass of sherry before they ordered their food. Valerie was happy with what Susana had ordered. They were waiting for the meal to be served and obviously Susana chattered this and that about the food and then as an after thought she said "Oh! by the way, according to predawn gossip the big boss is coming on Sunday evening." Valerie enjoyed the other girl's phrasing and then suddenly it stuck her that this `Boss´ was the same for her.

"Does Mr. Patterchinni have a flat in Berlin"? She wanted to know more about him, but at the same time her instinct warned her not to show much enthusiasm.

"No, no. Very rarely he comes here and even if he does he stays only for a few days and he prefers to stay in a hotel. But I heard he is looking for a house to buy. But my direct boss is Mr. Bismark who is highly efficient and runs the office smoothly."

"Does that mean he will be my boss too."

"Not to my knowledge. You will be working directly under Mr. Patterchinni I understood, because you have a separate office though in the same building".

"That's a relief" Valerie reflected. " Why?" the girl was really confused "Because you will be in the same building" Susana felt pleased.

The first course of the meal arrived and their conversation was temporarily interrupted. After the 'Guten appetit ´, from the waitress they began their meal. Sipping the wine and the sherry with an 'Mm` they started their dinner. They were, half way through the meal when suddenly Susana showed signs of nervousness. Sensing the change Valerie asked

"Is something wrong"? "Shh... don't turn now. But look at the couple sitting behind you at the corner table" She even spilled a drop of sherry. "I will look later but first tell me what is it all about", Valerie asked softly.

"He is the sensation in our office complex which is famous for the popular international companies. His name is Hans Hoffmann. A bachelor not attached to any one permanently. He is the Managing Director for one of the biggest companies and has a lot of influence in the government", she paused for a moment. Before she could continue Valerie interrupted" Is he your dream man Susana?"

"Oh yes, but so he is for many of them" she said dreamily and a feeling of curiosity invaded Valerie which urged her to turn round and look at the person concerned. She casually turned her head, but right at that moment he looked up and they stared at each other and their looks clashed. It was Valerie who broke away quickly. Turning her head and looking at Susana she said, "Mm He is quite attractive, but not to my taste."

"Really, What is your taste then"?

"Dark, tough and serious you can say"

"You mean the one that comes in those romantic fictions! You don't meet them in real life do you? How typical English you are!" she exclaimed and both of them started to laugh. Obviously it must have attracted the attention of the other guests for they saw a few heads turning. Then Valerie heard Susana gasp and say "Oh God!"

Confused Valerie asked "What is the matter"?

"Hans is coming towards us" she said, under her breath. Before she could say anything more Valerie heard a male voice saying "Hi! Susana! wie ghets"?, in German. With a blush she answered "Gut" in the same language. Then turning to Valerie he greeted her in German. Valerie did not know what to answer and she hesitated for a moment. In the mean time Susana recovered herself and introduced Valerie. "This is Miss Valerie Wilson from England Mr. Hoffmann. She will be working for Mr. Patterchinni in the new office from Monday. Valerie this is Mr. Hans Hoffmann, Managing Director for one of the biggest companies in

Berlin. In fact we are in the same building complex"

"How do you do?" he spoke in English while extending his hand to her. Valerie shook hands and said "How do you do"?

"Care to join me for a drink"? the invitation was casual

"It was kind of you Mr Hoffmann", Valerie carefully pronounced the name, "but I don't want to intrude your guest. Moreover you see we are half way through our meal". It was easier to refuse to a stranger. If he was offended by the refusal he did not show it." Enjoy your meal Miss Wilson". and then turned to Susana and said" see you" and left the table before joining his partner at his table.

There was a stillness at their table and Valerie noticed that Susana was just nibbling with the food and not exactly eating. Cursing the man who spoilt her appetite she quickly finished her food. She understood there must be a reason behind Susana's mood, but she didn't want to ask anything. The best thing was not to say anything she decided.

After lingering with their coffee for some time they left the restaurant in silence. Suddenly Susana had become very quiet. In order to break the silence Valerie said "That was a nice evening. Thank you very much Susana"

Susana did not reply for a moment. Then she said "Once I thought he was very fond of me. But that is over now. Sometimes the old scar hurts you know"

Valerie merely nodded her head. They talked very little on their way back except in mono syllables and the rest of the time Susana was preoccupied, and Valerie thought to leave it like that. She knew sometimes silence was the best medicine.

Susana dropped Valerie at the door step and waited till she saw the lights in her flat then tooting her horn she drove off. Valerie felt sorry for the girl. Is she still in love with this man? Strange she confined it to me who was a total stranger. But sometimes it was easier that way. `I wish I don't see him again´ she thought earnestly. When she changed to go to bed her only wish was ' I want to have a quiet day tomorrow.'

Chapter 12

As predicted Saturday was uneventful and Valerie slept till eleven because she had requested Susana not to bother to take her out every day. When she finished her bath, Valerie switched on the television. She could only see the German programmes. 'I must ask Susana about the English programmes. But for the present I have to be satisfied with this' she thought. She glanced through the packets in the fridge and decided to have a canned soup of asparagus. After drinking it she took some fresh grapes and sat before the television and watched an old film of Romie Schneider.

She did not know what woke her, the music from the film or the ringing of the telephone. It was already dark outside and she had no idea how late it was. At first she thought the telephone call was coming from the film. Then she realised it came from the room. Half sleepy and half confused she lifted the receiver and said "Hello"

"Hello. Miss Wilson, this is Quinn Patterchinni." her heart jumped.

"Oh, Hello Mr. Patterchinni", she didn't know what to talk. She had a strange feeling she had heard this voice before, but she soon put back the thought as groundless and paid attention to what he was saying.

"I heard from Miss. Klein that you have arrived. I just wanted to know if every thing was alright."

"Of course Mr. Patterchinni, it was very kind of her to meet me and bring me here." "How do you like the place?"

"You mean Berlin or the flat? because both are new to me. If it is the former I haven't seen much as for the flat it is fantastic."

"Okay, then we will meet at the office on Monday morning. I hope Miss. Klein made the arrangements to collect you. So till Monday, Good night" Valerie heard the click of the receiver before she could say a `Thank you` and a `Good night`. `Funny a boss calls you only to ask about the place´ she wondered. From his voice and the conversation Valerie could not come to any definite conclusion about the man for whom she would be working. She preferred to start on firm footing rather than scepticism. Curiosity warmed like a maggot in her body. It was hard to elucidate. Judging from his tone and manner, he could be either ebullient or purely showing professional courtesy. From all what she knew he appeared to be a reserved person. Valerie assumed the speed of her imagination as apriority and decided to stop her fantasy at that stage and wait till she saw him in person to give the final verdict.

We are distained to come in contact with certain people who will play a permanent role in our lives. Like natural catastrophe either it is a disaster or a narrow escape, but either way the reminiscences are painful. You neither want to forget nor remember. The big question was why in the first place it should happen. Fate, destiny, coincidence or simply life it self.

That was the very thought in the mind of Quinn Patterchinni. He never knew what made him to make that call. If he had waited for one more day he could have asked the same question in person. Quinn felt he was disturbed by the whole affair. For some mysterious reason his noble qualities left him for a moment and motions of combat took complete grip of him. Something triggered in his brain. He was instinctively aware of the urgency of meeting this girl and taking the sweet revenge. That settled, he drew himself away from the reflections and glanced through the window as though searching for the peace he would have afterwards.

The whole of Sunday morning Valerie spent on studying the map of Berlin and the whereabouts of her working place. It was thoughtful of Margaret to buy the information book for her before she left London. She could see that her flat was in the centre of the town and the new office within four kilometres. She will have some difficulty in the conversions. Especially in buying things Euros instead of Pounds. She felt a bit lonely without anyone to talk to. So far she did not get any message from Susana about the time she should be ready to go the next day. 'May be I should wait till Susana calls me.' She was thinking, when the telephone rang. 'Touch wood' she said loudly and picked up the receiver. "Hello, Is that Valerie" Margaret's voice was clear as crystal, "I did not want to disturb you on Friday for it was quite late when I returned. And yesterday I was busy with the teacher's day. How are you dear?" Valerie 's home sickness vanished, "Oh Margaret every thing is fine here, though I feel a bit lonely. How is daddy?"

"Fine. As usual he had gone out for a walk with Stephen from the church" there was a soft note in her voice when she said that. "Have you met any of the people with whom you will be working?"

"Only one, the public relation officer Susana. A nice girl of my age."

"When are you starting your first day dear?"

"Tomorrow. By the way the boss Mr. Patterchinni called me yesterday and said hello"

"How did he sound? Nice and young." 'typical romantic' Margaret, Valerie thought.

"Quite formal I should say"

"You can't judge a person in one day Valerie. Most of the men sound different on the phone than what actually they are!"

"Sure. Soon I will know when I meet him in person", Valerie had her doubts. Very often she had been proved wrong lately.

"Okay. I will call you when ever possible dear. Till then good luck"

"Convey my love to daddy when he returns from the walk, and thank you for calling, bye" Valerie kept the receiver. The moment she took her hand off the phone started to ring again. Before she could say 'Hello' She heard Susana's voice "Hello this is Susana. I tried to call you but your line was engaged"

"Yes my step mother called me from London"

"Did she? She sounds to be a caring step mother."

"Oh yes she is. I have known her for a long time before she became my step mother"

"That's nice. Otherwise how do you feel?"

"Fine. By the way Mr. Patterchinni called me last night"

"Aye.. that is something, and what did he say?" the curiosity in her voice was obvious.

"Well nothing special. It was just a short inquiry about how I feel and a curt good Night"

"That is typical of him, chatting is never in his agenda. Anyway a call from the boss is an honour I dare say"

"Oh yes", she said and then added "but any gentleman will do that"

"Well said, he is a gentleman" Susana emphasised the 'is' like a typical English person which is rare among the foreigners.

Valerie wanted to change the subject so she asked "Susana at what time you will collect me tomorrow?"

"Just like me. I called you to tell that I will collect you at Nine in the morning. Will it be alright?"

"Suits me and thank you"

"Till then Tschuss"

"Tschuss" for the first time since her arrival in Berlin she felt at home.

'I hope everything goes well tomorrow 'was the last thought before she drifted into sleep. But who could rule out the hands of fate.

Chapter 13

Valerie got up quite early the next morning. She filled the water and started the coffee machine, then she opened the windows and smelt the fresh air. She could see the whole street. Except the bakers all the other shops were closed. It was cool but not cold. The aroma from the automatic coffee machine drew her back to the kitchen. Drinking the coffee she recollected the events of the previous few days. She felt sorry for Susana. She hoped that the depression Susana had did not prevail when she comes to collect her. Finishing her coffee she decided to put every thing behind her and face her first day at the office with all her might.

She chose a powder blue suit which was neither too modern nor too old. Tied her hair up with a knot, wore a pair of sensible shoes with small heels, and a touch of lipstick of a paler shade was satisfying. Her pearl ear drops and her silver watch were the only accessories. She collected her coat and hand bag and was ready when the intercom sang like a bird announcing Susana's arrival.

"I am coming down, Susana", she voiced and at the same time closed the door of her flat. Without waiting for the lift to come she ran down the steps to the entrance. Susana greeted her with a bright smile. There were no signs of strain what so ever. Valerie was happy for her but did not want to comment anything. Both of them got into the car and fastened the belts.

"It will take only fifteen minutes from here to the office" she said starting the engine. "How lovely, then I don't have to get up very early", Valerie said, jokingly.

The traffic was heavy but Susana was a good driver especially with the left hand driving which was new to Valerie.

"You must give me some training for left hand driving Susana, before I try to drive in Berlin" she said. Susana smiled and said," You don't have to be afraid. I won't allow you to drive till I am sure you could really find your way in Berlin". Further conversation was not possible till they reached the main gate of the complex. Susana showed her card to take her car into the security area. And she selected a place where she could easily take the car out.

It was such a big complex that Valerie would have been lost if not for Susana. They underwent the security check with Video cameras at the main entrance before they could enter into the building proper.

"Daily routine you see". "Even for regular staff"? "Yes since a lot of foreign companies are located in this building especially the various media"

"That sounds interesting".

"I heard you were in the media. Don't you get such system in your country?"

"In fact not strictly for small private companies, and more over our office was only for our company, where every body knows every body". There was a sharp pain when she thought about the last visit to her office. "Here we go. Valerie beware of the wolves!", said Susana as the door opened for them to enter. " I am no Red Riding Hood", said Valerie. Both of them burst into laughter like old friends.

Valerie's appearance at her new office had quite an impact on both men and women working in the office. There were appreciation, hostile and inquisitive looks from the staff. Susana walked straight to the main office and Valerie followed her. She knocked at the door "Herein" said a German voice. Susana opened the door and Valerie went in. It was a large room, with all the look of an executive's office but somehow or the other one could not call it excellent. The cabinets were arranged on one side. There was a huge round table with some leather chairs. There was a coffee pot with cups and saucers, milk and sugar, some small bottles of mineral water and a few Cola bottles, turned down glasses on a tray with a few serviettes neatly arranged. On the left hand corner there was a vase of flowers obviously a few days old. Some plants, only green, were placed here and there. A map of the world showing the transmission wave lengths and an old painting which looked out of place were the only ornamental objects on the wall. Valerie's eyes turned to the middle of the room where there was a writing table made of solid teak on which piles and piles of papers were stacked. There was a slight movement behind them and slowly Valerie saw a short man fully dressed, rising from the revolving chair. She couldn't hide her disappointment. This is Mr. Patterchinni? Though she had no definite idea about him, this was not the picture she had in mind. The man rising from the chair had a face void of any expression. He was short for a man, quite fat with a prominent Hitchcock belly. Valerie was sure the button of his coat would never reach the buttonhole on the other side. He was bald except for a few grey hairs at his temples. Nothing moved except his lips when he spoke. On the whole a man whom you could not fathom. Before she could regain to normality a feeble voice said "Welcome to Berlin Miss. Wilson", and extended his hand to her at the same time, coming round the table. "I am Mr. Bismark the Director in charge for the Berlin Office", the relief Valerie showed did not escape Mr. Bismark's eyes, for he said, "I know you expected to see Mr. Patterchinni", he halted his slow speech giving the impression that it was more of switching to a foreign language than anything else. "He is delayed in the traffic. I just got his call. He asked me to receive you here and send you to the new office in half an hour. It is one floor down. "Valerie shook his hand and said, "How do you do Mr. Bismark.? And thank you for receiving me." He acknowledged it with a nod and at the same time releasing her hand. Then he turned to Susana and said," Why don't you take Miss. Wilson and introduce her to some of the staff with whom she will be working Frau Klein." Then turning to Valerie he said "Would you like to have a cup of coffee Miss. Wilson"? Understanding that he would prefer not to be disturbed, Valerie declined the offer by saying "Oh thank you Mr. Bismark but I just had my coffee at home. And I would rather go and meet the other staff." He nodded his head again and returned to his desk.` A man of few words' was her first impression. Seeing the dismissal

Valerie turned to the door. Then she heard him calling "Ah Miss. Wilson I am told that Susana will be working with you till you feel confident enough to work alone at your new office. That means Miss. Klein", he addressed directly to Susana, "You will be Miss. Wilson's assistant till she needs. You could shift your things today or tomorrow to your new working place. Miss. Müller will take your place." Surely Susana did not expect this for she said," I was not informed about it, Mr. Bismark."

"I myself knew it only this morning." There was annoyance in his voice. Clearly he did not like the change. He stared at Valerie as though the fault was hers. I have at least one person who doesn't like me, that's for sure, she thought when she closed the door.

"I don't know if this is a promotion.", Susana said more to herself, "But I am glad there is a change, which I badly need." Valerie was silent for a moment and then she said "I have a feeling that Mr. Bismark does not like me."

"He doesn't understand why a person from London should come to this office, when we have a totally efficient German staff. He is from the state Hanover you know. These conservative people hate to see any sudden changes without a good reason. He thinks he has the best offers" Susana raised both her hands, palm facing Valerie, shrugged her shoulders and said " I am not one of them" and smiled. This was news to Valerie.

"He can't be so rational. After all he is working for a foreign company. He can' t afford to be partial. Further more what does he know about my capabilities?"

Before Susana could answer they were in the down stairs office. Valerie was introduced to various people of different catogeries. Mr. Dirck Hoffman and Miss Meleni Schneider who were two of the editors, Frank Seeper and Katherin Thoss from the camera team, Ulrich Meyer from the graphics and some of the new recruits who were there. She could not judge any of them because they were very formal. One thing she understood. It was not going to be that easy to communicate with them on equal terms. All through the introductions Valerie kept a smiling face which was one of her greatest assets.

Susana said "Miss. Wilson we could go and sit in the lounge till the boss comes, if you want." Valerie was astonished to see the sudden change in her tone, but did not comment about it till they were out of ear shot. When they were absolutely alone in the lounge, she asked, " Why did you call me by my surname?"

"I don't want anyone to think that I am familiar with my Chief. We have to work here even if I don't work for you,. "she said pleasantly but making Valerie to understand her point. Very often there were these `false friends´ mixed in the English spoken in Germany and Valerie understood she meant her boss. ' Well I must remember that personal relationships are out of bounce in the office' Valerie made a mental note. Then remembering her own panic she asked, "Susana What kind of a person is Mr. Patterchinni."? She was shy to ask about his appearance. "I don't meet him everyday. But the few times I had met him he behaved as a perfect gentleman. But boy! he is a man to look at! May be the Italian touch. But he is a rock as far as women are concerned. No current affairs in Berlin. They say he must be having an Italian girl friend because very often he gets calls from some one called Patricia in the last few months. They speak in Italian and some times in English. We suspected there is something because he receives these calls only in his private line I heard. But the girls working in his office are crazy about him except Jasmine the only one who is sensible enough not to dream on things that cannot be obtained. She is Turkish and happily married" Susana took a pause before she added, "Isn't it strange you didn't meet him at the London office, because he spends most of his time in London and Italy, and I heard it is a very big Company"

It was more of a statement. But for Valerie, a question she herself had asked for the past two weeks. "I was interviewed by his secretary Miss. Johnson and Mr. Patterchinni was quite busy at that time she said." Valerie defended. "Well high time we go and confront the Italian master" Susana said throwing the butt of the cigarette she was smoking and walking towards the main office.

Chapter 14

'It is good that I meet this girl without Martin Bismark's hawk eyes. Nobody should know my motive for having her here' thought Quinn Patterchinni while struggling through the Berlin traffic. His eyes were heavily blood shot from lack of sleep. "This girl is getting on my nerves. And I can't sleep till I have a revenge for Gina's death". His face was grim. `Sooner or later Gina would have done the same' peeped a voice within himself. But what ever the situation was, this Miss Wilson was directly or indirectly the cause for my sister's death, and I want to make amends by making her feel unhappy in every possible way. Especially she should know the feeling of losing some one whom you really loved. I don't know how and I don't know when but I know that I will'. He vowed to himself. There was a sharp pain in his heart when he thought about his dear sister Gina and her sad ending a few months ago. He couldn't do much when she was alive because she did not confine anything about her unhappiness to him till it was too late for him to ameliorate in any way. Before he could do anything at all the unfortunate incident happened and Gina took her own life without giving him a chance to make things better for her. And all because of this stupid woman who made a report about something that she herself, was not sure. He thought about the happy times Gina and he had together.

Their mother left them and died in an accident, when they were only eight and ten years old. From that time Gina was the only family he had apart from his father. And now of course Patricia. When he thought about her, his anger reached its peak, and the hatred for Valerie increased that he pressed the accelerator as a reflex action despite the fact that he was quite near the office complex.' The quicker I do the better' was his thought when he entered his office. Very often while trying to punish others we punish ourselves. But seldom do we realise that.

There was no sign of anyone waiting at the outer office. The receptionist greeted him with a cheerful smile, "Good morning Mr. Patterchinni!"

"Good Morning Miss Wagner. If Miss Klein comes with the new member of the staff send them to me." He avoided the newcomer's name. He collected the post at the desk an action he normally didn't do and walked towards his room.

"In fact they were here and had just gone to the lounge. At any minute they will be here Mr. Patterchinni." 'The way this girl pronounces my name!' At the beginning itself he never allowed any one to call him by his first name. Even Mr. Bismark addressed him like that.

He smiled and turned slightly and said "Well then they could come to me directly."

He felt some kind of stormy intensity. Suddenly he sprang to life and walked quickly to his room and sat down in his chair cursing himself for this treacherous sort of liquid excitement. He was opening one of the letters when he heard a knock on the door. He paused for a moment to compose himself before he said "Come in." Opening the door Susana entered first and then he saw her.

Valerie halted at the entrance for a moment distraughtly. 'Oh no not him'!. For a split of a second she thought of running out of the room. Since Quinn did not show any kind of recognition, she advanced forward ignoring the trickle of sweat at the back of her neck. Susana did not notice any of those and she simply said "Good morning Mr. Patterchinni, Here I am reporting for duty." Then seeing a blank look on his face she added, "Mr. Bismark told me that I am transferred to this office"

"Ah Yes" he said with a vague recollection, but his gaze did not linger on Susana but passed beyond her and stayed where Valerie was standing. Realising her duty Susana said "Oh I am sorry, I have brought Miss. Valerie Wilson whom you are waiting to meet." Quinn stood up with his full six feet and came round the table to meet Valerie. Although his feelings were different, with a hint of humour he said, "So we meet again if I remember correctly." Susana blinked and looked from one to the other. To bring an end to the confusion, Quinn said " Though at that time we did not know we will be meeting again am I right?". Valerie realised it was high time she spoke and said "That's for sure." Her heart was thumping and she was afraid it could be heard by the others.

"Welcome to Berlin Miss. Wilson." Quinn extended his hand to her. Valerie could feel the warmth flowing from his hand. She imagined he held her hand a little too longer than needed before he turned and greeted Susana.

"Please take your seats"

He was decidedly formal and sitting down in one of the chairs Valerie had a feeling that he was stronger and deeper in character than he appeared to be. Unaware she developed a pronounced frown which did not go unnoticed by her employer, for he said " I know your first day in your job could be tiresome and full of anxiety, especially if it is in a foreign country. But I hope you will slowly pick up the threads as days go by", he looked at her expectantly. He did not want her to retreat now, not after all the trouble he had undergone to get her. Realising the ball-game, she sprang to life by bringing a bright smile on her face and said, " On the contrary I like challenges Mr. Patterchinni. I only hope that our encounters in the past did not give you a wrong impression about my capabilities." "Not at all, I rely on Miss. Johnson's judgement when she selects a person to work for my company". 'You liar' said his heart.' So you did not choose me', reflected Valerie. Both of them seem to have forgotten that there was a third person in the room.

It was the tinkling of the bottles reminded them of Susana. Quinn became aware of his forgotten manners and said, "I am sorry for my bad manners." He apologised, "What would you like to have? Please make yourself comfortable till I get the papers for you to give an idea of the work you will be doing Miss Wilson", and walked towards the big cabinets. Susana took three glasses and poured cola for the first and the second seeing Valerie's nod and looked up and asked "What would you like to drink Mr. Patterchinni?". He turned slightly and said without looking up "Mineral water if you don't mind please". When he returned with the papers the intercom buzzed and he pressed the button and asked "Yes Miss Wagner", he listened for some time. Then he said "Tell him to call me after one hour, by then I will be free. In the mean time I will send Miss Klein to the airport." He retraced his way to the table where the two of them were seated. For the first time he looked at Susana and said, "I am sorry Miss. Klein, there seems to have been a mix up with the dates and one of the men from my American office had just reached Berlin and you have to collect him from the airport. Would you mind"? Susana stood up leaving the half finished drink and said "Not at all Mr. Patterchinni."

"Thank you. but first you finish the drink. There is no hurry, he could wait for a few minutes longer. Miss Wagner will give you the details as to where you should find him" Susana gulped the rest of the cola and said, "Alright I'll take my leave" and got up from her seat. She shook hands with him and Valerie, concealing a sigh of relief. Departure of Susana was the last thing Valerie wanted and she looked at the departing figure helplessly. She could not think that it was a coincidence. Slowly she turned her head and found herself staring into a pair of eyes that had the most mesmerising power she had ever experienced. What is this man trying to do to her? In order to evade further contact, she took her glass of cola and sipped. To his surprise Quinn felt the same effect during the contact but at the same time he remembered why she was here. All the tenderness vanished and he became hard as a rock. He took out the papers from the folder and spread them on the table so that both could see them clearly. Then he looked at Valerie directly and said in a serious tone, "Miss. Wilson I want to launch a new project at the beginning of next year. That is in almost less than three months. Nobody had tried this before and that means I have to risk both money and the name of the company. That doesn't imply that I have no idea about the project. But it should be kept confidential. That is why I wanted some body from London and some one who has little contact with the media and other companies in Berlin. I hope you understand my reason for employing you for this project.", his attitude was positively docile." I want you to have the minimum association with people who are otherwise inquisitive to know about my project. Any decision will be taken between you and me." There was no better way to make a person feel important and he did it very smoothly. The less contact she had with other people the better. For the first time Valerie opened her mouth " Does that mean that I don't discuss anything with anyone other than you"

"Exactly, all the others working here will help you with the language and other minor work. The real paper work should be kept confidential. The only way to avoid any trouble is to keep away from any of the open parties and to go out with people who are connected with this kind of projects", he paused to drink some water. Is he giving me a chance to ask questions? Valerie wondered.

"Why do you trust me?" He seemed to be taken aback by this question. Then suddenly he smiled and said, "Call it instinct." Valerie took it with the same humour and said "Well if you say so."

She knew it was not the truth and he knew she did not swallow. Still she continued the conversation. "And how do I find out the good and the bad?"

"I trust you are intelligent enough to distinguish between the wolf and the sheep Miss. Wilson"? ` Right now you are sitting with one of them ´a cynical grin appeared on his face which Valerie took it as a challenge.

" You seemed to think that I should know all kinds of people Mr. Patterchinni. Thank you for the complement but one could always make a mistake in judging a person"

"So you agree that you could make a mistake"

"I never deny it"

"Mm. That's interesting. Perhaps it is a protection for some mistakes you will commit in the future or is it something to do with the past"

"Well I have not committed any serious mistakes in the past, perhaps as you said a protection for the future."

`Not now, any false move would give her a warning, and I don't want her to know about my plans till she swallows me hook, line and sinker.'

thought Quinn revengefully. Bringing a broad smile on his face he said " I think we are looking far beyond the future Miss Wilson, let us stay in the boundaries of the present."

Amazed by his tact she filled her face with an attractive smile by which Quinn was carried away for a moment. Concealing his momentary feelings, he concentrated on the papers that were before him. Once they started to discuss the work concerned, nun of the personal feelings crossed their path. The rest of the hour was mostly spent on Quinn's talking and Valerie listening, except for an occasional question or two from Valerie. They were almost coming to a close when the intercom buzzed. Walking towards his table he pressed the button and said "Yes, Okay. I will take the call." There was some delay on the other side. Then she heard him say " Hello Bob! How was your journey? I hope Miss. Klein met you" He listened to what the other person was saying. He must have heard something funny, for he laughed heartily and said" I won't mind provided you meet me at my hotel at 8 o'clock. So long." He kept the receiver still smiling? He could be handsome and nice at times' Valerie's face softened with a dreamy smile.

She was shocked by her cogitation when Quinn turned and asked, "Day dreaming about your boy friend back in London?" He did not know what instigated him to ask such a question. But Valerie thought it fair to tell him that there was no possibility of her leaving the job on the pretext of matrimony. " I am more interested in my career Mr. Patterchinni" Valerie's face was serious when she said that. "Oh I see", he looked at her with an expression which contradicted his statement, for more than understanding there was relief on that. Misinterpreting his reaction she added "If I take the responsibility I would never go back except under extreme situation. You don't have to think that I am one of those individuals who value emotional issues to that of moral obligation."

Quinn was speechless with that out burst for a second. `She is a spit fire and I have to handle her carefully` But at the same time he wanted to shout back and ask about the moral obligation she had forgotten a few months ago, instead he said "I am glad to hear that." Valerie felt small by his polite answer. She looked up at him and said " I am sorry, I shouldn't have spoken like that." But Quinn only chuckled, and waved his hand putting an end to the conversation. When he spoke again all his tenderness had vanished and he became more business like." Ah Miss Wilson, I have a list of companies who could give us the estimate for the requirements of our company. Please call them and find out the details and if possible tell them to fax their quotations. If there are difficulties in understanding any of them get the help of Miss. Klein. Regarding the prices consult Mr. Bismark in my absence. One thing you must remember. The price in Germany is not always lower than London. "He clearly indicated that he didn't like follies and nonsense.

"I have asked Miss. Wagner to give you a separate room so that you could work there without much of the disturbances and distractions of the outer office. If there are doubts you could always contact me. You may take these papers but please remember to return them to my table before you go even if I am not here. "he pressed the button in his intercom and said "Miss Wagner could you please come and take Miss Wilson to her room" It was a clear dismissal for Quinn bent his head on paper work and looked up only to nod when Miss. Wagner came to collect her then continued with his task. When she turned he said as an after thought" Miss. Wilson, you don't have to work the whole day today." She could only say "Thank you". Clutching the papers she came out of his room with mixed feelings. It was evident that `Mr. Patterchinni had no time for any female outburst and he will never be moved by any platonic emotions´.

Sometimes one predicts the future without knowing it. Especially it is a common knowledge a hasty promise under provocation is often difficult to keep up. But the irony is people continue to do that. It is here that a supernatural force takes the destiny in its hand deviating the natural course in the most unexpected direction.

Chapter 15

Later on when she was settled comfortably in her new room she vowed she would never behave like that in future, especially in the presence of Mr. Patterchinni. Keeping that in mind she started to work earnestly with the work she was assigned to do. The outer office was empty when she came out of her room to find her way to the rest room. Being new she had taken the wrong turn when she collided with a dark haired girl who was definitely not a German. The girl smiled brightly and said" Hello, you must be the new assistant for Mr. Patterchinni." She had a strong accent. "Yes " replied Valerie." I am Jasmine Asadulla from the corresponding department. I assume you are on your way to the rest room, because if so, you are in the wrong territory. This goes to the studio. Please come with me. I don't know why you didn't ask some one at the reception." The last sentence was more to herself. "I think they all have gone for the lunch break" Valerie said. " No, they must have gone for the meeting in the big hall to plan for the annual party", she supplied the information.

"What party?"

"Even for a small thing they have a party. But this is the biggest party they have each year. I don't normally stay till late, so I am not interested in the planning also." The look she gave was one that gave her identity. By now they have reached a turn and Jasmine pointed out the sign board to her. Thanking her Valerie took her leave. Jasmine replied with a smile.

Re entering the main office Valerie noticed Mr. Patterchinni's door was ajar. And she could not help over hearing part of the conversation freely floating out side... Patricia Darling, I promise you I will be with you for Christmas" a short pause, then "You know I don't forget you"...I love you too. God bless you my Darling" Valerie heard the click. She started to move towards her room. For no reason she was irritated for she thought 'Why can't people keep their private talk within closed doors instead of letting half the world to know´. She felt something within her dying. Was it her spirit? When she returned to her seat she could not continue her work. Actually she was staring out of the window when the outer office became active again with people.

Half an hour later Miss. Wagner came and said." Miss. Wilson, Mr. Patterchinni said Miss. Klein would not be able to take you back and I have instructions to take you with me." So he does not want to talk with me to show where I stand. ´I get your message sir`, she wanted to shout. Then she realized that was neither the place nor the time to show her feelings. "That's kind of you Miss. Wagner, I need some time to get used to the travelling. I hope it is not out of your way?" Valerie asked politely. " In fact it is, but I don't mind. My sister lives closer to your flat, you know. Besides Mr. Patterchinni expects orders to be obeyed", she said with a meaningful look. Valerie did not make any comment. In a place like this one never knew who was a friend and who was a foe. Especially she was new and had no firm footing either in her job or with the people.

At the very same time Quinn was standing near the window smoking a cigarette with a lungful of smoke and struggled to let it out. What ever hell he had slipped into he alone could come out of it. When? It was a question even he could not answer.

It was ten minutes to two when Valerie prepared to leave the room. Taking the papers in her hand and the notes she had prepared she went and knocked at Quinn's door. "Come in," Valerie opened the door a little wider and entered the room. His eyes were closed and there was sadness on his face which was not there in the morning. Valerie cleared her throat, but before she could talk he said "Keep the papers on the table Miss. Wilson" When she neared the table he suddenly opened his eyes and looked at her with a mixture of hatred and confusion. Valerie felt a bit nervous with the power of his look that she almost dropped the files with a k1op.To overcome her tumult she simply said "Since Miss Wagner is taking me back I must leave now"

There was a sudden change in his attitude when he said "I am sorry it was an emergency. Please let me know the moment you are ready to drive by your self, then you could have your own car. By the way Miss. Wilson I hope you come at 9 o'clock tomorrow so that you could clear your doubts if you have any before I leave for Italy tomorrow. Something urgent has cropped up and I had to make a short visit." "If you could outline the work I should be able to finish when you return. I will do to the best of my ability, Mr. Patterchinni." Her voice was flat. It was Quinn's turn to be puzzled. 'Now what have I said or done to get such a curt reply 'wondered Quinn. 'Don't I know the reason for your urgent visit. May be your darling Patricia wanted to say 'Hello' Valerie boiled within herself. `Surely you have a bee in your bonnet 'echoed her senses.

"Well if you wish" Quinn paused, "I will outline them tomorrow." It was Valerie's turn to blush. "Oh I am sorry, May be the first day nerves" She tried to smile, but the smile did not reach her eyes. Quinn nodded his head that he understood with a cynical grin on his face. She could not stand that and at the same time she heard her name being called by Miss. Wagner so she excused herself and said "Excuse me Mr. Patterchinni May I go?"

"Well I see that you are in a hurry to leave than stay" he raised his eyebrows waiting for an answer. When he did not get one he said "Good afternoon, Miss. Wilson"

"Good Afternoon Mr. Patterchinni" she said humbly and came out of his room.

****

She was still feeling furious with herself for her behaviour. Leaving the room was the only dignified thing she could think of doing. That was the second time today she had annoyed him. What was the matter with her? Where was her sweet temper for which her father was proud of? When she walked out of the office with Miss. Wagner to the parking place she was not happy with her first day at the office.

Quinn stood up from his chair and walked to the window. He lit a cigarette and drew a lungful of smoke. He was so close to the window that his breath misted the glass. It was uncharacteristic of him to show temperament. But today everything was different. This woman and Patricia drove him to two different directions. Above all the message about his father's deteriorating health and his urgent request to come and see him had upset him a lot. Gina's death was a blow to the whole family and worst of them was his father, for whom she was the pet, till she married Haward and went away. This delayed shock was worse than the initial shock for the old man. If only Gina had confined to him he could have prevented this disaster which had shattered the harmony of his family. Quinn himself did not want to settle permanently because he was afraid he might make a wrong choice and thereby make his father unhappy. There were times he had some involvements but nothing serious enough to lead him to the alter. In his old age all his father needed was love and devotion from his children. The last time he spoke with the doctor he indicated that his father's days are numbered, may be a year or two. The big Villa with all the luxury could not give senior Patterchinni the happiness that Patricia gave him. He ate with her, he talked with her and spent every minute he was awake just sitting with her. He had such devoted servants like Maria and Vichinni. But who could replace a wife or a daughter. Some times he even called Patricia 'Gina'. But how could a small child spend her time like that without playing with children of her own age. Quinn knew the pain and suffering he under went when he lost his mother at a very early age. And now Patricia. All because of this stupid...

He turned his attention to the super model figured Valerie who was just opening the door of the car. When she was out of reach he had a different feeling but after seeing her and talking to her he was confused. To say he was out of his mind was an understatement of considerable proportion. She is beautiful definitely, she is a spit fire without a doubt, capable, yes, she is calculative. why not? She is lovable, certainly. Suddenly he imagined how she would react if he kissed that sensuous mouth passionately. A wicked smile appeared on his face. Well that will be the sweet punishment for her when I return. "Was it a punishment or a desire?" He did not tarry to analyse his feelings further. Perhaps if he had, he would have been surprised.

Chapter 16

Returning to her flat Valerie had similar thoughts. She laid down on the sofa without changing. Why should this man have such an effect on her. He did not refer to their previous encounters in London. Does that mean they were accidental. If so how was that he remembered them. She on the other hand could neither treat these encounters lightly as she knew very well the dynamic effect he had on her. Those piercing eyes and the aristocratic nose and the dimple on the cheek and the unusual gesture of lifting one side of the upper lip. She giggled at her thoughts. What would it be to be kissed by him? For a moment she was dreamy, dazed and romantic. Abruptly she put a full stop for her wild imagination and faced the reality that he was a man who was engaged to be married to his Patricia whom he loved deeply and passionately. Deflated she got up and went towards the kitchen when the door bell rang. Wondering who it could be, she pressed the intercom and said, "Who is that?" No one answered. She was about to turn when she heard the bell again. This time it came from the door. Valerie looked through the peep hole and found a young man with a bunch of flowers. Thinking he must have made a mistake, she opened the door to say so.

But the young man greeted her in German and said "Blumen für sie Frau. Wilson" with a bright smile.

'Flowers for me'. Valerie asked "Are you sure?", "You are Frau Wilson?" he asked in mixed German. "Yes", "You see card Frau" he spoke in broken English and showed the card attached to the bunch. Valerie opened it and read aloud "A belated welcome to Berlin. QUINN" The young man did not wait as they do in the hotels. From her face he understood that it was a surprise for this lady and as she did not return the flowers, he turned and ran through the steps whistling. Valerie closed the door and leaned against it for some time, holding the flowers close to her heart. The white, yellow, orange and pink roses. Why this sudden change of attitude! She walked to the kitchen with dreamy eyes and placed the flowers in water. It's a pity she did not know his private telephone number. How will he react if she hugged him and thanked him. Maybe he just felt sorry for me being alone in a strange country. There could be a thousand and one reasons. I should not come to any conclusion. Maybe he had already forgotten that he sent the flowers. With these thoughts in mind Valerie was having a bath when she heard the telephone ringing. Just wrapping a towel she came and picked up the receiver.

"Hello! Is it Valerie", Sally's voice said.

"Oh Sally. I am glad to hear you. How are you?"

"How are you?" asked Sally. "I called Margaret and father and they gave me the number I waited till the baby went to sleep. Are you home sick?"

"I was, yesterday. But not today. The office is huge and the people are nice though they are a bit passive. Well I can't expect people to like me on my first day"

"I am glad you like it. Have you met your boss yet"

"Of course. Mr. Patterchinni is very kind and I have a flat of my own."

"Well he sounds old"

"On the contrary he is an Italian bachelor, and quite handsome"

" Hey, hey you are not already in love with him"

"He has no eyes for women, besides his girl friend is in Italy with whom he is very much in love."

"You sound positive", Sally said with disappointment.

"Sally you are not yet a grand mum to do match making" Valerie laughed. Sally laughed too. She talked for some time and then called off.

Valerie was preparing to go to bed when the telephone rang for the second time. Thinking it must be Susana she answered "Hello Susana"

"Sorry to disappoint you" said Quinn quietly. Valerie stopped dead for a moment. "Miss Wilson are you still there?"

This time Valerie spoke. "Yes Mr. Patterchinni," After a small hesitation she said "Thank you for your flowers. They were lovely. ", there was a sound of a glass on the other side.

"You are welcome. Excuse me I am just having my nightcap." he was searching for words. "I wanted to convey a message from Miss. Klein."

'No wonder you called, so it is official again' Valerie's spirit took to a down hill. This time when she spoke her voice did not betray any feelings.

"Well I am listening" There was a pause before he said, "She has to go to Frankfurt with Bob to look into a property that I very much wanted for my company and would not be able to collect you in the morning." Before he could finish Valerie offered

"I don't mind coming by a taxi Mr. Patterchinni" There was a chuckle on the other side.

Then he said "Only now I saw that my hotel is not far from your flat and if you don't mind I will pick you up on my way to the office"

Valerie's first instinct was to decline the offer, but then he said "I thought I could take you and show you the proposed project site so that it will be helpful for you to work on it in my absence. Once the new building is finished we will be moving to this place for the production" Now he waited for her answer. Did she have a choice?

"As you wish Mr. Patterchinni." There was a flat note in her voice which was quickly noted by Quinn

"Then that's fixed. I will meet you sharp at eight Miss Wilson. Good night."

He did not wait for her good night. Valerie had an empty feeling and the prospect of meeting Quinn the next day did not appeal to her. He is a business man and he wants the maximum from his employees. That's that! Slowly she drifted into sleep.

Valerie's entry:

First time in my life I decided to write all what I feel and hope to continue

in good times and bad times only on a special theme 'Love'. Today is a special day in my life. Some kind of unknown pleasant feeling I have which existed never before. Some people we meet and forget some we remember, but only a few we cherish. I think, Quinn will become one of those few. The moment I saw Quinn again, I felt as though I had known him all my life. The first hand shake was brief and I looked down at his hands. Those long fingers and the manicured finger nails were the first thing I admired. Some thing in my heart said I love this hand I don't know anything about this man. But I love this man.

`Close your eyes, give me your hand, and feel my heart beating.´

******×*************

Back in the hotel room it was Quinn who was wide awake. After Valerie left the office Quinn felt it was not fair on him to make this girl work on the first day itself. He could have been a bit kind to her, after all he is a good employer all these years. The pain he saw in her eyes when she left had haunted him and, when he was passing the road where she lived it had made him to stop the car and order that bunch of flowers. He could not give a reason for this impulsive gesture. Why was his anger not as intensive as it was in the beginning. Within a day he was obsessed by those beautiful and expressive eyes.' Quinn wake up old man. You employed her to take your revenge and not to become a prey of her beauty.' Warned the other side of him. 'Don't be silly. After taking all the trouble of finding her I am not going to forget my aim. A slow torture is more painful than anything else. I am only going to pretend that I am falling for her, so that I could hurt her'. But it was a dangerous game he was playing. He did not see that the weighing scale of his plan was moving more towards the opposite side.

Chapter 17

The next morning Valerie woke up by the sound of the alarm. She had a quick bite of bread and ham and a cup of coffee. She searched for a suitable dress to wear for the day. She had noticed that most of them who were working there wore some thing black or related to black and she could be easily picked up by the people in the complex as a foreigner with her choice of soft colours, typical English. Valerie did not want this distinction, especially in her office. You did not feel at ease when people stare at you or stop talking when you pass them. She felt more like an intruder than a co worker. At the entrance, in the corridor, at the parking place, she felt as though she was walking under deep scrutiny and that kind of 'pins at the back' feeling made her self conscious. She had appeared on the TV knowing that her audiences were always anonymous, but this was like facing live audience. Her boldness in her job did not totally erase the normal shyness she had which became of her. True, the business brain of hers was an asset and she had attended a whole lot of conferences and business appointments but they were different. Either they were all the same category or she knew most of them. But this was a different country and almost all of them were strangers. So the best thing was to become a 'Roman' she decided. Secretly enjoying the thought she chose a black striped mini skirt and a white blouse, black shoes and a tiny black ear studs. The reflection on the mirror was that of a business woman. Nothing personal or private. She took the light coat in her hand and turned from one side to the other a typical action most women did to be satisfied in the three-dimensional effect. Face, front and back not neglecting the side pose. It was then that she saw the bunch of roses. Quickly she went and changed the water. Something within her wanted to keep them as long as possible. She caressed one of them with full of tenderness and fearing she might crush them she withdrew her hand. She was still in a daze when she heard the door bell. She made a quick movement swinging her coat and then it happened. The vase toppled and the whole thing came down and she tried to catch the vase and landed on the floor with the water, flowers and the vase falling on top of her. The whole dress was ruined and part of her hair wet with water was hanging pathetically on the sides. It took some time to get over the shock and then when she got up she had a sharp pain in her ankle.

One shoe sprawled at a distance and she removed the other and taking it in her hand, limped towards the door. She was only an inch away from the door and she heard some one knocking on the door. She opened the door dangling the shoe in her fingers. "One of your kind neighbours..." Quinn stopped half way through his sentence and burst into laughter. At that moment she felt the lowest of the low. Weakened by the loss of the flowers and the shock of the fall, Quinn's laughter was the last thing she wanted. Leaning on the wall she gave a groan which put an end to Quinn's laughter. He quickly came in and shut the door. Then rather earnestly asked "Miss Wilson what's the matter?" His seriousness alerted Valerie and brought her back to her senses. She remembered that the man opposite her was none other than her Boss and she was supposed to go with him to have a look at the site officially. In order to overcome the embarrassment she had caused by the whole situation, she said "I am sorry there was a small accident Mr. Patterchinni. If you could give me ten minutes I will get ready"

"Are you sure it's nothing serious?" He was concerned. Valerie was rather slow to respond. But feeling the importance of an explanation without causing any alarm she replied "No, no. A vase of flowers fell on top of me when I was trying to save them. Unfortunately I slipped." This time her voice sounded almost normal.

"Well take your own time, Miss. Wilson, I don't have an official appointment."

He was so charming and did not get irritated by the delay. This surprised her. She tried to overtake him by squeezing through the narrow space between him and the wall finding the shoe in the hand a hindrance

4TH DIMENSION OF LOVE

she raised it above her head. The finger slipped and it landed on Quinn's foot. Bending and taking the shoe he said "We seem to be destined to meet with a dangling shoe" remembering quite vividly their first encounter. When he lifted his face it had an empty smile, but Valerie could see a tension hidden behind the smile. She thought better not to reply, instead she said, "Mr. Patterchinni please make yourself comfortable. Can I offer you something to drink?" she asked politely. She couldn't see his face when he said "Never mind Miss. Wilson, if you get ready as quickly as possible we can go to the site." Valerie could not understand the reason for the change of his mood. But walked to the bathroom and quickly washed her hair and dried it. She had no time to choose a dress carefully.

Her green silk suit was the first thing that came to her hand and she wore it. She let loose her hair because it was not totally dry. Tying a scarf round her neck she wore almost flat shoes this time. Taking her hand bag she came out of the room. Quinn was still standing with his back to her. The vase of flowers was back on the table. He must have done it while he was waiting for her. Or did he think she would fuss over that and waste some more of his valuable time in cleaning. He must have heard her move for he turned and there was a kind of appreciation in his eyes which was soon replaced by a blank look. "Ready?" The question was mechanical 'So he wants to play cool So do I' Valerie marched to the door without glancing back. But Quinn overtook her and held the door open for her to go out. Then closing the door with the minimum of noise he extended his hand for the keys Valerie was having in her hand. He secured the door, took the key and gave it back to Valerie like a perfect gentleman.

Quinn was preoccupied when he followed her to the stairs for which she was heading. He was thinking the day he met Valerie for the first time and how he hated her. 'But now' he tried to dig his feelings. The intensity of it had quite subsided. He had a vague feeling that some thing else was happening for which he had no control over. He could not ignore the effect of her proximity that shattered him both physically and mentally.

He cursed him self when he missed one of the steps.

Valerie was silent till she got into the car, then thinking it would be rude to continue like that, she said "To which part of Berlin we are going Mr. Patterchinni?

"More towards the south. An area called Tempelhof. During the occupation of the allied forces in Berlin, before the wall came down, the Americans had their Air Force Base there." His reply was curt. But Valerie pretended not to notice that.

"Will I have a chance to see the wall or rather a portion of the wall, for they say it has been totally removed."

"Well there are portions of the wall in some places especially near the Reichstag, that is the former Hitler's Parliament now rebuilt with a modern touch, or the newly built wall at Check Point Charly in the former American sector. But I am sorry we won't be able to see that today."

"Oh", Valerie sounded disappointed.

On an impulse he said "Perhaps I will take you there one day." Quinn did not know what made him to say that. But Valerie was indeed surprised and turned to him and said, "That's kind of you".

Quinn slightly tilted his head to look at her and the piercing look of his went deep into her heart and made her blush. Quinn certainly did not expect this reaction. He felt a strong urge to kiss that beautiful mouth. When this urge and common sense clashed he turned his eyes and focused them on the road. Valerie lowered her eyes with a deep frown which he saw through the rear view mirror. Both of them were silent. By then, they had come to the end of the high way and Quinn turned his car to his right where the sign said 'Tempelhof'.

They drove scarcely a minute or two before he turned into a road where a construction was sited which was almost in the finishing stage. Quinn parked his car in front of the name board said QP Enterprises. He came round the car and opened the door for Valerie to get down. Valerie swung her legs round and got out and he closed the shutters and locked the car. Something prevented her from walking parallel to him. So she walked ahead and reaching the entrance she did not know where she should go. Compelled by the need she turned and looked at Quinn who was a few feet away from her. The morning sun was from the correct angle to give a special glow to her face. The slight tilt of the body gave though not a perfect side pose but revealing enough to give her perfect figure to its advantage. The mouth which was asking to smile or not to smile, the inquiring look of the eyes and the loose dark hair disarranged by the gentle breeze, Quinn simply drank the beauty. Valerie did not guess what was in his mind purely for the reason that her own thoughts were in similar tracks and she was stunned by the handsome face that was darker due to the light effect of the nature and the smartness of his dress and the walk that blended. It was Valerie who broke the spell by asking "Where do we go?" "To your right" he said concealing his disappointment of not having enough time to admire this walking beauty to his content.

Once inside he was welcomed by the main supervisor and others working on the construction. After brief introductions they were taken on a conducted tour of the building and Valerie was engrossed by the explanations given by the supervisor. Quinn was always in the background watching every move of hers. By the end of the tour they were taken to the VIP lounge and Valerie sat down in one of those comfortable chairs with a sigh.

"Tired?" Quinn asked tenderly.

"A little." she replied.

"Would like to drink something?"

"Yes, Please."

"Hot, cold or strong?"

"Cold drink,"

"Lemonade?"

"That's fine"

Quinn turned to one of them and spoke in German. They did not have to wait long. A tray full of drinks came with a lot of ice cubes. Passing a glass of iced lemonade to her Quinn took a glass of mineral water. Now he seemed relaxed and was talking to the supervisor. Suddenly he said "Miss. Wilson will be coming here occasionally to see the work in my absence." Because the information was new to Valerie she looked up at him only to be warned by a nod from Quinn.

Though they were friendly in manner, they spoke very little in English, except of course the chief supervisor who spoke English with a German accent. Valerie could manage her German but she felt shy to talk before the natives and Quinn's presence did not make things better. Having a degree in Economics helped her to understand various things they were discussing about the contracts but some of the them were talking rapidly in German and that was difficult to understand. Quinn noticed the occasional frown appearing on her face and repeated them in English for which she was grateful. One by one the staff returned to continue their work and in the end only the chief supervisor remained. Quinn looked at his watch and said "It's time we make a move?" He shook hands with the supervisor and Valerie followed suit and they came out of the building fully relaxed or that's what Valerie thought till she found out that Quinn was rather silent on their way to their office. They had travelled for five minutes in silence. Then suddenly he said "I am sorry about the proposition of you visiting there in my absence. I wanted to tell you about it sooner or later. Due to certain commitments I had to leave Berlin quite often. And I want you to take some responsibilities of the project. Today I will out line what and what you have to do when I am here and also in my absence". He was business like and serious. None of the light heartedness which he exhibited at the site was visible. "Yes it is easier to work when I know what I am expected to do Mr. Patterchinni." It was just a reply any sensible person would have given in her place. It was strange that his moods were unpredictable. One moment he enjoyed a joke and the other moment he kept her at a distance. Some times the tenderness he showed was overwhelming and some times he used hard tone for no plausible reason. Valerie was still trying to solve this riddle when she heard him say "Here we are". As though she was wakening from a dream she sat up. Then she noticed that they were in the premises of the building complex of their office at the parking place reserved for QP.

This time when he stopped the car Valerie made sure she closed the shutters before she got down. A smile escaped from Quinn's lips. At last his mood had changed 'But how long' wondered Valerie. When she came and joined him he said, "I will bring you to the entrance of the office. Since I have something urgent to attend to, I have to go back"

"I think I can manage alone Mr. Patterchinni. It is really not necessary that you should accompany me"

"No, no I don't want to take a risk of searching for you all over the complex when I return. I will make sure that you arrive safely in my office."

Valerie did not protest further. While walking he asked, "I want to give something special for a young lady in Italy. What would you suggest Miss. Wilson"?

Valerie knew whom he meant and said "A perfume or a piece of jewellery would be ideal" "Perfumes I rule out, yes, a piece of jewellery is a good idea. Thank you" he smiled. So Patricia had enough perfumes from him and other modern gifts are too common and he wanted to give her some thing special of course, especially if she was young as he said. She had heard that some men like to marry women who are very much younger than themselves. So he is not an exception in keeping up the tradition. Her trail of thoughts prevented to spot Jasmine near the entrance. But Quinn did. He said "There you are Miss. Asadulla" rather loud. Jasmine turned and beamed with a smile. She had taken some extra care on her appearance Valerie noticed. "I had to go back again so please take Miss. Wilson with you. I dared not allow her to go on her own fearing she would take a wrong turn", he sounded relived. "Good morning Miss. Asadulla" Valerie, greeted the other girl. "Good morning." Jasmine said and turned to shake hands with Quinn jingling the bangles in her hand.

Quinn took his leave and walked back while Valerie and Jasmine waited for the lift. "Were you out on a business appointment" asked

Jasmine. "Not exactly. Mr. Patterchinni gave me a lift to the office and on our way we went and saw the new site ", Valerie told the truth. "Yea, I heard that Susana is otherwise engaged" she smiled slyly. Valerie did not answer. Then there were other people coming in the direction of the lift and that put an end to their conversation. When they reached their floor Valerie was busy getting out of the lift and did not notice Hans Hoffmann in the passage. She saw him walking towards her only too late. "Hello! Miss Wilson. How are you?" this time he took care to greet her in English. "Fine, thank you" Valerie preferred to move on, but he was actually blocking the way. He must have sensed her impatience for he gave way and said "See you" and went in the opposite direction. When he was out of ear shots Jasmine said "You know him Miss. Wilson:?" "Only a casual acquaintance at a restaurant" she replied curtly. But Jasmine had no intension of stopping with that. "Please be careful with him. He has a habit of capturing beautiful women and play with their feelings. Susana was one of his victims you know" Valerie pretended she had not heard. But Jasmine continued, "Susana worked for him before she came to QP". They were approaching their office. " And you know... "Jasmine started and Valerie cut short by saying, "Miss Asadulla I am not interested in other people's affairs. If you don't mind I will take my leave here as I know you have to go to the other entrance. And thank you very much." she shook hands and walked towards the door without looking back. Jasmine stared at her. Well the temperament did not match the English rose she thought sardonically.

Chapter 18

Miss Wagner greeted Valerie when she entered the main room. Greeting her back she opened her room. Today it was looking better she noticed. With some plants installed and some expensive furniture replacing the older ones. Sitting on her desk she started to arrange certain things, remembering to bring some of her personal things to keep on the table. Then with the help of the computer on the table she tried to get some data while waiting for Quinn to give her further information. The best way to spend the time was to do some serious work she reflected. She did not notice the time till she heard the outer door open and Miss. Wagner greeting some one. That deep voice definitely distracted her. But she continued with the work she was doing. She heard the telephone at her desk ringing.

"Miss Wilson speaking". "Miss. Wilson, could you come to my room in half an hour's time. I have a few telephone calls to make and after that I am at your disposal." The clipped voice of Quinn was clearly authoritative and official. None of the softness that was in the morning could be seen. "Yes Mr. Patterchinni", her voice was equally non committal. "Thank you." There was a click.

Valerie badly needed something to drink, and came out and poured some tea for herself from the table where the glasses cups and spoons together with the coffee flask, tea flask, water and fruit juice were set for the employees. They were the same like that she saw in Quinn's room except that the crockery in Quinn's room had quality. Most of the staff must have taken coffee because the lid was lying on the table. "Would you like to have some coffee? ", asked a friendly voice from her left. It was a young man with a leather jacket whom she had not met before. She shook her head and said " No, thank you, I prefer tea " She smiled back. He looked more of a trucker than an employee at the QP Enterprise. And

Valerie for no reason, disliked men with short leather jackets. So without wasting her time further, she took the cup of tea and turned to go to her room. The front door buzzed and with the cup in the hand and facing the opposite direction Valerie could not see who was coming. The others in the outer office did not pay much attention and continued with their work. Balancing the cup in one hand she pushed opened the door of her room. When she closed the door she heard Miss. Wagner's gasp and an all round "Oh", which sounded like an admiration. 'I am not an inquisitive teenager', Valerie over ruled the desire that cropped up to open the door to see what was happening. At the same time she heard the buzz of her telephone. Carefully placing the cup of tea she answered it. "Miss Wilson I have finished with my work, you may come in please." There was a change of voice as though he was stifling a laugh when he added "Bring your cup of tea with you." She was sure she heard him laugh. A feeling of anger whelmed up within her. What was there to laugh about if I drink a cup of tea. She purposely took the cup in one hand and the papers on the other hand and tried to open the door. Failing to do so, she held the papers in her mouth and opened the door.

In the middle of the outer office stood a big package. Miss. Wagner and the others were fussing around it. Slowly taking the papers from her mouth, Valerie looked at them. Frank was walking towards the packet with an open knife most probably to cut the cord. When the packet was opened it revealed, two cases of champagne and a beautiful cake with a lot of pastries and chocolates. Valerie did not know the reason for such a treat, innocently she asked "Are we celebrating somebody's birthday today"? All the eyes looked at her in surprise. Then seeing the look in her eyes Miss. Wagner asked "Guess whose?" with a mischievous grin. With a hint of humour Valerie said "Not mine", and they all laughed. The atmosphere was that of a family celebrating a house party. Valerie remembered her appointment with Quinn and started to walk towards his door. Before opening the door she asked " Oh please tell me who the birthday baby is." Suddenly the door opened from inside and Quinn said "I am." Embarrassed, she blushed and a creeping sense of shyness came over her. Her voice faltered and the lips trembled. Clearly Quinn enjoyed her embarrassment and all the others joined by bursting into laughter and, she found that behaviour quite impolite. Valerie had only two possible ways to hide her face. Either into the chest of Quinn who was standing almost touching her or to drop the cup and the papers and cover her face with her hands. Since both were not possible she stood there transfixed. It did not take much time for Quinn to realize it. So he stepped into the room giving enough space for her to enter.

There was 'Happy birthday' and somebody singing in German language, a "Thank you" mixed with more laughter. Once inside Valerie felt better. Accepting all the greetings from the staff Quinn came in at last and noticing Valerie still standing with the cup, he smiled and said, "Now you can sit down Miss. Wilson."

Valerie said, "Sorry about that"

"For what?" He looked at her inquiringly.

Valerie replied shyly, "For not knowing about your birthday before hand."

"It's not your fault. Nobody will expect a person to know the birthdays within two days in an office." But something within him wanted to hear her wishing him so he added, "Won't you greet me at least now!"

"Many Happy returns of the day Mr. Patterchinni!"

"Here in Germany people kiss the birthday baby", she heard him say. Valerie pretended not to have heard and concentrated on arranging the papers on the table. As he went round the table Quinn had a deep frown. 'Why should I have such passionate desire to hold her and kiss her when I should hate her with all my might.' He couldn't find the answer or was it that he wouldn't want to answer. There was an uncomfortable silence in the room and it was Valerie who broke it by saying "Mr. Patterchinni if you could brief me the work I am supposed to do in your absence, I would be grateful, for I see we don't have much time left" She drew him into polite conversation there by cutting any possibility of facing unnecessary delicate situation. `I don't have time for his rainbow coloured moods´ Valerie thought. Flinching with guilt Quinn bent his head and started to concentrate on the papers before him.

Valerie had written in her neat hand writing what they needed and Quinn took his pen and marked the important ones and said "I think you better note these things on a paper before deciding the company. We have three major requirements. The telecasting charges of the studio and the personals, the pros and contras of satellite and cable transmission before we decide on one of them, and the materials we have to buy and we have to produce. Recently I met one of my friends who is a consultant in this kind of affairs and he strongly believes that satellite transmission has better prospects than cable transmissions. Especially with the introduction of the digital, system." here he paused and looked directly at her as though he valued her opinion. Now she was being safely led into the field which she had plenty of knowledge. "I have a strong feeling for digital system and the satellite. I thing if we take this chance it would be profitable. Especially with the new companies producing the digital recorders wanting to catch the market." Quinn was intrigued by her. 'One thing is for sure. This girl knows her job'. He pretended to turn the pages before he answered. "I had the same thought and a five year contract would reduce the price by twenty five percent. So you could contact either the German Telecom or the French Eutelsat for the beginning. But there is no harm in inquiring the Sky Channel from your country." He measured her. When she did not respond he continued, "Although the American firms are trying to get introduced in Europe according to my estimate it will take another year or two for them to fully establish." The smile he had was blank. Typical business-man's reaction. 'But he can't deny I am not a nobody'. A feeling of determination took over her. Quinn felt rather than sensed it. "Most of such negotiations are done by well known consultants who are known to both the parties and they have certain understandings between them. I have learned this in the past. That is the very reason I want you to do the talking to lead them into confusion." He paused rather to take his breath than to search for words. Valerie knew it was wise to keep quiet when experienced people were talking. Even a fool was thought to be clever when he did not talk. But as for Valerie, she needed time to assess the matters. She looked at him expectantly, so he continued, "I have good confidence in your capabilities Miss. Wilson. But I would like to give you a piece of advice. In Germany if we foreigners try to prove ourselves smart they become smarter. So it is always good to be aloof on certain matters. This is some thing I have learnt during the past few years." He sounded genuine. `This man can pick up any colourless wire in the web of business. No wonder he is successful´. Taking her silence as his advantage he continued, "You always bargain with them mercilessly, and then you get a compromise that is profitable. But before you make an appointment with the firms concerned please let me know so that I will make myself available" Seeing a frown appearing on Valerie's face he quickly added, "Not because you can't really deal with the situation but I would like to see how you deal with it. Nothing like watching in person than hearing about it. " Is he being sarcastic or was he challenging that her gender always needed a male moral support in big affairs. Well she would prove him what she was capable of doing with or without him. The rest of the time was spent on choosing different firms and planning the schedule for the coming month to deal with each section. It was almost Two O'clock when Quinn showed signs of restlessness. There was a knock on the door and he said "Come in" with a subdued yawn. Miss. Wagner came in with two plates full of eatables together with a bottle of champagne. Placing them on the extra table she asked, "Are you available for your callers now Mr. Patterchinni?" So he had given his orders. She fought back a wild desire to laugh but tried to hide it by biting her lip. "Yes for the next half an hour" he smiled back at her. There was a fleeting exchange of understanding between them, when she saw a sheepish grin lingering, on his face. "Would you like to have coffee or tea?" Miss Wagner asked looking directly at Valerie. "I would like to have some tea if possible" Valerie replied politely. "No problem", Miss Wagner walked out of the room closing the door. "A typical English habit" muttered Quinn. "And what is the Italian habit?" Valerie couldn't resist asking. "Eating Pizza" came the prompt reply. The telephone at his desk buzzed and she got up from the place and walked towards the door. A bit of fresh air would do her good. As she closed the door behind her she saw the whole crowd in the office enjoying the treat given by Mr. Patterchinni. Somebody was telling, "The chief is not in a mood to celebrate his birthday".

"Why"

"I don't know, But I heard recently there was a death in the family, and he is very attached to the family "

"Is it his mother? "No, no, sister"

This information was news to Valerie. She understood the reason for his moods. May be he was attached to this sister. She even felt angry with herself for being unfair in judging him. She felt sympathy sprinkled with tenderness. She saw Miss Wagner preparing the tea. She went near her and told "Let me do it. Mr. Patterchinni is busy on the telephone and I have to wait till he finishes the calls. You please come and sit down." "As you please". "Would you like to have that lovely piece of cake?" Valerie tried to be friendly. Miss Wagner thanked her and sat down while Valerie brewed the coffee for Miss. Wagner and a cup of tea for her. She was really hungry. Strange she did not feel hungry when she was working. She had heard a lot about the wonderful taste of German cakes, and tasting them was a privilege. The outer office was more of a get together room than a working place. Valerie sat and observed what was happening. Time must have run and she realised that only when she saw Quinn at the end of the room making his way towards her. Valerie drank the tea in a gulp and went towards him. They met half way through and Quinn retraced his steps. She had an odd feeling that all of them were looking at them but she dared not look back. Quinn kept the door open for her to enter the room. And the whole, ordeal made Valerie a bit nervous. As she closed the door she heard some one saying "Ah the English rose." She could see Quinn stiffening. As she sat down, she had a vague feeling that among those people out there some of them did not like her. As though reflecting her thoughts Quinn said "These Germans still have a bit of hostility to you English people. But strange they don't have the same feeling towards the Americans". As he said this he was thoughtful. "I hope no one treats you in that way in my absence". She couldn't fathom his feelings." I have asked Bob to keep an eye on you in case of emergency". He looked at her as though waiting for her approval. "There is no need for that Mr. Patterchinni. Your fears are without any grounds". Valerie did not want to be treated like a helpless teenager. "Well it's only for an emergency", Quinn was happy that she did not jump to the idea of a male company "I could always call Susana if she is in town". "That's exactly I what I say" he grinned". From what I understand Susana and Bob are always together. Bob simply fell in love with Susana, so asking Susana's help is virtually asking Bob." "How nice" was the only comment from her.

Soon they resumed the work they were doing before. But Valerie's mind was engaged otherwise. She felt slightly embarrassed that she could not give Quinn at least a birthday card. She had already noticed some beautiful packages lying on his table. Then she thought about his sudden departure to Italy. Any man would like to be with his fiancée on such a special day. But the way Quinn referred to his journey it sounded it was not previously planned. But that is Love. When you are near you want to be away and when you are away you want to be together. She imagined an Italian beauty coming running and hugging him and giving him passionate kisses hard on that mouth. A beautiful smile escaped from her which immediately turned into some kind of unknown pain that her mouth gave a twist. Quinn observed that' cloud hidden sun' effect and admiring the changes on that beautiful mouth he whispered "A penny for your thoughts" Coming to reality Valerie said " Not too pleasant." "Anything personal?" " Much too personal "

"Care to share them"

"Oh no". She cursed herself. Why should she often appear to be vulnerable before Quinn. Quinn's train of thoughts were in a different track. Did she really lie to him that she was not emotionally attached to any one. That smile definitely showed the traces of love and the twist in the mouth was some unpleasant thought or act or both. He couldn't resist thinking over and over again to find a suitable answer. Suitable for whom? Again they were silent, pretending to be busy with the calculations. Frustrated with his present mood Quinn made a move and accidentally the packages on the table were knocked down by his elbow.

Spontaneously both of them bent to catch the packages and Valerie a bit quicker. Catching them in both her hands she lifted her head only to see Quinn's face very close to hers. She tilted her face and doing so she bent slightly forwards and Quinn's lips narrowly escaped a collision with hers instead his lips brushed her cheeks. The romantic day dream a few moments ago combined with the physical contact in a sensitive place by that very mouth made her heart thump madly, lips tremble and pulse race. Quinn saw the blush that was spreading all over her face. How sweet and vulnerable she looked. To his surprise his whole body became electrified and charged. 'Since when did I become susceptible for the feminine charm and contact?' Quinn wondered. Though the whole thing happened only for a few seconds, the after effects were felt longer by both of them. Valerie's mouth opened slightly showing the brilliant set of teeth and her eyes still had the shock of the sweet memory. Quinn on the other hand felt an over whelming desire to hold her in his arm and feel the silky skin. If only people could do what they feel like doing all the time, the world would have been a paradise he thought wistfully. The time they took to recover from the shock and come to the existing world was not more than a few minutes. This time Quinn could not sit at his place so he got up and walked to the window and stared out.

Misunderstanding his reaction for despise Valerie wished that the earth would swallow her before he turned. Quinn on the other hand wanted to regain his normal posture before he faced the person who caused this situation. Being a man he was the first to control the feelings and when he turned there was no trace what so ever to the feelings that were tormenting him. In fact he appeared totally under control.

"Miss Wilson I think we have done enough for one day. You could take the rest of the day off"', he was not looking directly at her when he said this. It was a clear dismissal. Without giving an answer she started to pack her things. Quinn regretted the way he had handled the situation. The immediate forlorn look that reflected on that lovely face made him to feel guilty.' She looks like a wilted flower' he thought wryly. The word' flower' brought back the memory of those roses he saw at her house.

"Would it look silly if I send another bunch" But another voice within him said, "What are you trying to do to this girl. Is that the way to take revenge on a person." Those conflicting thoughts were still flying to and fro when he heard "Good day Mr. Patterchinni", and at the same time the door closing.

Chapter 19

Once outside his room Valerie regained some of her balance and walked towards her room. The brisk walk she had would have looked quite normal for the people working in the outer office. But Valerie felt as though some one was laughing behind her back. She opened the door with shaking hands. She closed it and leaned on it for a few minutes. She couldn't understand herself. A change that was not present yesterday was there. But she couldn't say exactly what it was. Was it anger or hopeless love? Valerie was never affected by any other man with whom she had worked with. There were a lot of them who tried to draw her attention in a serious way. But she never felt anything like this. Though she was still vague she knew it was dangerous and the sooner she got out of it the better. Having this in mind she walked to her desk. It was then it stuck her that she needed a transport to go home. She dialled the number of Miss. Wagner and asked her to order a taxi in half an hour to take her home. She spoke in the most natural voice. There was a slight delay for a reply. Then Miss. Wagner told "Miss Wilson, Mr. Patterchinni just rang and told me to take you home so I am getting ready. Give me five minutes and then I'll be ready to take you" Valerie hid her surprise and said, " It is not really necessary Miss. Wagner. It was kind of Mr. Patterchinni but I can manage with a taxi" "No Miss Wilson, this is his order and I prefer to carry out". Well that was neither the time nor the place to show her temper Valerie realised.' She is a foreigner in a strange country, in her new job which was only two days old, and she is not going to gain by rebelling against something which appeared to be normal in the eyes of the others'. So she released an empty laugh and said," You are the boss" and laid the receiver thoughtfully.

Should she thank him for his kindness? But in the present mood Quinn was the last person she wanted to talk to. She decided to leave it like that. She collected her hand bag and tidied the table a bit and came out of her room. Miss.Wagner came and asked "Would you like to take a piece of cake Miss Wilson, we have plenty of them". "I would love to" she said looking interested. "Though I am in favour of the chocolates "she added with a laugh. Did she fancy a movement inside the door that was ajar. "Well, I have the same weakness", said Miss. Wagner smiling. They were about to open the outer door, when Valerie heard her name being called. She knew the owner of the voice. She took a moment before she turned her head slowly to look in that direction. Quinn was standing there with a beautifully packed package. "I forgot to give this to you. It is from Susana", his eyes looked directly into her eyes. She couldn't read the expression in them, but it certainly conveyed a message which she could not understand. "Thank you Mr. Patterchinni." He simply nodded and turned away. Hurrying behind Miss. Wagner, she noticed that the package had a KaDeWe sticker. She knew that it was the most expensive and the most popular departmental store in the city of Berlin.

The drive from the office to her flat was unincidental, and promising to pick her up in the morning Miss Wagner sped through the evening traffic. Valerie opened her door of the flat and secretly wished she had her own car so that she could explore the city. She wished she had some friends whom she could visit. The first thing that entered her mind was to have a bath, then she looked at the package in the hand. She kept it on the table and took the piece of cake to the dining table. She put the coffee machine on and went and started to fill the bath. She removed her clothes and got into the bath robe and waited for the tub to fill. The coffee machine gave the signal and she collected her cup of coffee, and slowly drank it thinking about the events of the day. There was an unusual restlessness within her which she recognised and couldn't give a plausible reason. Seeing enough water had run, she went and closed the tap. Leaving the half drunk coffee on the table she went and enjoyed the bath. When she came out of the bath it was almost seven in the evening. She put on a fresh night dress and sat on the sofa and switched on the TV. She had no desire to watch a film so she scanned through the programmes and found the types of programmes she really planned to do in the future. Though some parts of the programmes were not to her taste it was not too bad. She even smiled when the moderator said "Last but not least" in English. Time must have simply flown for she soon found herself looking at the eight O'clock "Tagesschau" the news.

****

Sitting and waiting for the flight Quinn hesitantly dialled Valerie's number. He felt he wanted to make sure she was alright by hearing her voice.

He had no particular reason to call so when Valerie said "Hello!", there was a short pause before he said "Hello Miss. Wilson! I have another half an hour to kill before my flight so I thought of calling you."

Valerie almost dropped the receiver. Then she heard him say "I hope you enjoyed the chocolates."

"Chocolates? I don't understand". She was confused.

"Didn't you open the package that I gave you?!" he sounded surprised. "In fact I didn't", Valerie was apologetic.

Suddenly Quinn said "Do you have something to write? I forgot to give you my telephone number. In case of emergency you could always call me."

"That's kind of you Mr. Patterchinni." He could feel a soft caress in the voice or was it his imagination. He repeated the number for her to write. He checked and double checked. Then he said "In a day or two you will get your car then you don't have to depend on others. His voice was extraordinarily soft and Valerie felt as though she had a physical contact with him. When he did not hear a reply he said, "We have to do a lot of work when I come back"

"Yes I understand" Valerie did not want to prolong the silence. "Oh one more thing.", he said "The chocolates are not from Susana so please don't go and thank her"

"I don't follow" Valerie was really confused.

"Since I heard you telling, you preferred chocolates to cakes, I thought I could give them to you as my birthday treat.", there was so much of unexplained feeling in his voice. Valerie did not know how to react to that.

"Don't make me feel guilty. I couldn't even give you a card." she really felt bad. "Don't blame yourself. It is not your fault. Okay, it's time for me to go now. Good night Miss. Wilson." he whispered. ".Good night" she said and as she kept the receiver down she whispered " Quinn".

Valerie's Entry:

> Today I looked at his hand again while he drove the car. I love them. I could not resist looking at them. I wanted to touch them. I sent a signal to the hand and whispered 'I love you. "This feeling is slowly gripping me. I feel better talking to Quinn directly in my own imaginary world. Only two days and I am in love. Love is a healthy sickness they say and I agree. The normal reaction I show in the public is totally different from what I really feel. This is the same when I am with Quinn. That is why he can never guess what is in my mind. His birthday was a pleasant surprise for me. If I had known I would have given some thing in crystal just to show my clean heart which is empty, except him in it.Next time I will talk with you directly Quinn. I am sure I will feel better that way.

`and whispered `Happy Birthday to you´

Valerie had a restless night and she must have gone to sleep out of shear physical need. The next morning she was almost late to the office. Miss Wagner had waited impatiently till she was ready. Apologising for the delay she climbed into the waiting car. In order to forget the turmoil within her she concentrated on the work. But the absence of Quinn was felt in the office. During the break she was able to understand how much respect they all had for him. In the afternoon Susana came. It was obvious that she was in love. What a difference it made to fall in love and to be loved. A special glow in the face a twinkle in the eye, a gentle swing in the walk, and a dreamy smile it all added to the beauty of being in love. Bob was polite to her, and requested her to ask any help if she wanted. Then he said "Quinn told me that we should make arrangements to send a car for your use till he comes back. I have brought it and parked it. Do you think you could manage of your own. If you want, Susana would show you the map and explain to you how to reach the office safely. Won't you Susana?" His voice had a special softness. Susana was prompt with a "Yes of course" answer. All three of them sat together in her room and Susana showed her how to reach the office from her place. Then added, "Today we will lead you and you can follow us in your car. Tomorrow you could try alone. If there is a problem park the car and give a call to Miss. Wagner, she will come and collect you". She went down to have a look at the car. The car was in excellent condition Valerie was happy that she would be independent and would not have to trouble other people. Bob showed her how to handle it and warned her not to forget to lock the car when she parked it. She did a trial run with both of them and came back. Susana and Bob bid good bye promising to come back at five o'clock and drove away.

Valerie entered the room with a smile on her face. She went to her room and started to go through the estimates for the project. The first estimate was cheap but the facilities were limited the other one was expensive with rather a lot of special offers and the third one was reasonable, one could say. Yet if not for the high price she would have chosen the second one. Suddenly it occurred to her' why not put a try. She called the company concerned. "Hello, I am Miss. Wilson calling from the QP Enterprise. May I speak to Miss Christiana Roth the Marketing Manager Please?" She asked in German. "Einen moment bitte" There was a short delay and then she heard a soft voice

"Christiana Roth" Valerie switched on to English.

"Hello I am Valerie Wilson from the QP enterprise. I hope you speak English?" "Yes, Miss. Wilson", there was a renewed enthusiasm in the voice.

"Well I just called to say that your quotation is just a bit higher than the other ones. And I am sorry to say that we have to reject it." It is always good to attack them than to plead with them. Valerie's trick worked. The lady on the other side was fully alert for she said "Miss Wilson could you please give us some time to think about it.Our boss is away in Holland. He will be back tomorrow morning. As soon as he comes I will contact you." Valerie knew from the tone that the lady is more than interested in the contract. But she should play cool.

Clearing her throat she said, "In fact we have already decided to this other company. Unless or otherwise your second offer is much more tempting Miss. Roth." Her voice showed some authority.

"I will not forget that hint", Miss. Roth laughed, then as an after thought she asked, "What kind of difference is that if I am not asking too much" 'Well, well you think you are smart. I will play the ball' Valerie smiled.

"It's not fare that I reveal such things openly, but believe it or not it is quite a lot." Must not say at the first request.

"Is it over a million?" she was trying to trap her.

"You may call it", Valerie wanted her to know but not directly.

"You will hear from us, say...in two days time. Could you wait till then." She wanted to make sure.

"At the moment Mr. Patterchinni is out of Berlin. We plan to sign the contract with the other company as soon as he comes".

" Please give us a chance to renegotiate the proposal Miss Wilson "Now there was a plea in her voice.

"Nothing is in my hands, I could only do what Mr. Patterchinni says. But if you promise to send your second offer as you said then I can delay the things a bit Miss. Roth. " Valerie knew the time had arrived for a compromise.

"You will hear from us I promise. And thank you very much Miss. Wilson for your help." There was a triumphant note in her voice.

"You are welcome." Valerie was satisfied with the out come. If the offer comes before Quinn returned well and good.

Time had run so quickly for Valerie and when Susana knocked at the door at ten minutes to five she was still reading some of the files connected to the project. She packed the files while chatting to Susana and took them to Quinn's room. She made sure that the door was locked and gave back the keys to Miss. Wagner. It was not until she was in the corridor with Susana it struck her that the company concerned was none other than Mr. Hans Hoffman's company. But knowing the involvement Susana had with him and the present affair she had with Bob she thought it was not wise to mention anything to Susana. Even clearing a doubt. There was plenty of time for her to collect any information she wanted she reflected.

When she followed Susana through the traffic filled roads of Berlin her thoughts were otherwise occupied. The Mercedes glided through the streets. She did not have any difficulty in driving that. She registered some land marks in her mind so that they may help her to find the correct way to and f r o to the office and her flat. When they reached her flat Susana tooted the horn and sped away waving her hand. Valerie parked the car carefully and remembered to lock it. Today she was in a happy mood and as soon as she entered the flat she switched on the radio. They were relaying a concert from the Philhamony the famous concert hall for classic music in Berlin. She called her father and spoke with him for some time with the usual affectionate way and inquired after Margaret when she heard that she was out. She could feel that her father sounded satisfied with his new married life. After a short dinner she tasted some chocolates which were given by Quinn. Did they taste better!

When she went to bed she couldn't sleep. She thought of various things that had happened within those two days. But every time the memory of Quinn came in between them. At last she drifted into sleep with Quinn's laughing face.

The next day Valerie was able to come to the office without much difficulty and she congratulated herself for not making any mistakes. When she walked into the office she felt a different atmosphere. People were looking at her curiously. There was a hush in the main room which was broken only after she closed the door of her room. What ever the cause, Valerie was not really feeling uncomfortable. After settling in her room she went out to get the keys to open Quinn's room. Again the same silence followed her till she returned to her room. Valerie thought it was better to ignore that than to notice. But she wished she had a friend in Berlin. She had little to do with the others in the office. So she spent the lunch break in her room but came to get some tea from the outer office. This time she could see a few smiling faces. That's better! a rueful smile tugged at her lovely mouth. She heard a soft voice "Sie ist wirklich schön" meaning 'she is really beautiful'. Was it a comment made on purpose. Valerie pretended she didn't hear that and continued to walk back. Once inside the room, she decided that she would try to have a normal relationship with those who are working in the office. The day passed without much events and Valerie returned home light hearted. She wanted to go out for dinner but changed her mind and prepared some salad and sat before the TV. But her thoughts were miles away. She visualised two people a man and a woman young and beautiful holding hands and walking on the streets of Rome. She had almost a choking feeling. For no reason she felt sad.

Valerie's entry:

I have an emptiness because you are not at the office Quinn. When I heard that you have an Italian girl friend I did not feel jealous.I only thought how lucky she is. I simply want to sit with you and talk like yesterday. Only two days, but I feel that I eat with you and live with you. I do not have any cheap thoughts like the others who are in love. This is a special love and I want to keep like that.I don't hope- then I will wait, and I don't wish- then I will expect .From the bottom of my heart I am telling you. I have no expectations. It is a very special love that I thought never existed till now. The happiness I have can't be expressed. It is shear bliss.

`Do you feel the same?´

Chapter 20

"You should know both I and your sister made a great mistake of being ruled by heart and faced the consequences. I am sure you would have realised it by now." Senior Patterchinni was lying on the bed in that private hospital where all what money could buy was provided. His face was pale and the wires that were temporally detached on his request for his beloved son's visit were hanging on the sides of the bed. He hated to look vulnerable before his son. But the amount of equipments around him spoke the story of his health. He tried to adjust his head position by shifting his abdomen a bit higher, holding the chain hanging above his head. Quinn moved to help, only to be signalled to be seated. Quinn resettled in his seat which was close to the bed. Mr. Patterchinni looked at his son with pride. when he talked there was a seriousness in his voice. " I am sure you have passed that kind of blind love stage. I know you travel a lot and have the chance to meet variety of women. I had that experience " he paused just to recollect those memories with a mischievous smile. That look lingered when he continued to say " There is no harm as long as they are thought only as experiences and not life itself. One thing you should understand, home is the haven, and I will be happy if you could marry a nice, pretty, Italian girl and settle down in life. Besides..." he paused to stifle a cough into a half chuckle, " Patricia must grow up here in Italy and it will be better your future wife lives here and not roam around" 'It's not fair´ Quinn wanted to say but thought about the doctors warning and nodded his head. His father signed with his shaking hand the need to drink some thing. Quinn poured some water and passed it on to him while thinking "I am the only consolation he has and I should try to do, all that I can to make him happy.' but he was not sure. Forcibly bringing a smile to his face" he replied. "The problem comes only when I marry. Till then you have nothing to worry Papa". Only in the most intimate moments he called his father 'Papa'.

"It is easy to pull down but difficult to build," said the old man, " I loved your mother very much and still I do. And only I know the misery Quinn" he closed his eyes as though recollecting the bitter sweet memories once again.

The old man felt the warmth of his son's hand and an affectionate squeeze. He slowly opened his eyes. Allowing a smile spread on his wrinkled face showing he understood and shared his son's devotion. The freckles on his nose were a bit darker due to the age when the light fell on him from outside. Neither of them spoke but sat in an almost congenial silence until the older man looked at Quinn appealingly and asked "Do you think the past had been forgotten, dropped into a place where memories don't follow?", He grimaced at the last phrase.

Quinn saw the nurse signalling at a distance that it was time for the patient to have a rest.

"Papa why don't you relax and get some sleep." he concurred avoiding with equal skill any direct address, "It's enough for today." And the old man said "Yes they are only bright nothings" he paused to catch his breath and whispered "The curse never ended, it continued with Gina my lovely girl" The sadness seen on those eyes was so intense that Quinn closed his eyes gritting his teeth.

He knew over the months this had swelled and expanded by repeated retelling. With motions grown, circumscribed by age, the old man simply shook his head "If I don't talk now I'll never." Suddenly there was an intake of breath when he asked "You are not in love?" It was more of a statement than a question. Quinn recognized the manoeuvre aimed at putting him for a confession. He hesitated only for a moment and said "I have always shared my goods and bads with you, and you can be sure I would not dare to marry someone of my choice or for that matter anyone without first telling you. So please relax and go to sleep." He waved his hand to the nurse who came to take over. Bending his head he kissed the old man's hand, a habit from childhood, and left the room.

Walking through the corridors of that private hospital, Quinn was feeling depressed. There were lines across the handsome face. He just had a long talk with the chief doctor about his father's health condition. There was no immediate danger but he was rather feeble and one may never know, after all he was a heart patient. The doctor left it open.

Chapter 21

Quinn's thoughts flew back to the days he spent all the hours possible, with his father, learning everything he could. His father was a shaken man after his mother left him. But he recovered from his initial shock and concentrated on developing his business.Quinn and Gina were too young to understand what was happening. Servants were silenced by the senior by firm orders. No one ever talked about the lady of the house.An innocent question like "Where is Mama?", was totally ignored by papa and became a taboo among the servants, that Quinn and Gina stopped asking the question. Apart from the servants there was an aunt, a distant relative of Mr. Patterchinni. Many of the English customs they had learned were either changed or overlooked. By the time Quinn was seventeen he showed quite an interest in television productions, his father's business. Mr. Patterchinni had confidence in his son that he sent him to America for further qualification and training, only after he promised to return to Italy to continue his business. Quinn was an ambitious young man and followed his father's advice. During the eight years in America, he learned all about media and had some good contacts in Hollywood, that his father was proud of him. The short time entanglements he had were not taken seriously by his father as long as they were passing affairs. But the unfortunate thing happened, when he took Haward on a business cum pleasure trip to his home country Italy. Haward was a young film producer wanting to shoot his film in Italy. Well it would be a boost for their firm thought the Patterchinnis, and contracts were signed. Gina's arrival from Switzerland's finishing school was a celebration for the family, so it was not a wonder that they invited Haward for Gina's home coming. It was love at first sight for Gina. They never realised it was ill timed. By now Haward knew the Patterchinnis, their popularity, their wealth, their influence and he did not hesitate. He not only allowed the bait merely to float, but flicked at the line in order to bring the fish closer by showing passionate reactions to Gina's every move. Whether the shooting of the film progressed or not the love affair did. The hardest task was to convince the Senior. Gina usually demanded than requested. And after long discussions and arguments with the support of Quinn and the encouragement from Haward she was able to convince her father. In the end Gina won. On a sunny July morning the proud father gave away the charming bride to Haward making him to promise not to take away his daughter from Italy. When Patricia was born Haward was busy with another film and he was becoming more and more popular world wide he scarcely had time to spend with his family. Since he had his head quarters in London, he more or less became a resident there. The passionate Gina missed him a lot. Seeing Haward occasionally gave no joy, and when the situation became unbearable, she decided to go and settle down in London. When it finally came to open Haward supported the old man openly and encouraged Gina in private. Seeing the misery of Gina, Quinn intervened and made an appeal on behalf of Gina and requested his father not to be too hard on Gina. At last when Gina left Italy with full of hopes, it shattered the happiness of her father almost killing his spirit.

****

Mr. Patterchinni had said something about a letter that arrived from Gina's lawyer in England. Though he was interested to see that his first concern was his father. He loved the old man and he was grateful for all what he had given to him. He did not bring Patricia with him because the old man wanted to see him alone. Just before he left the room his father repeated "Quinn boy it is high time I see a grand son who will one day inherit all I have. Why don't you get married to one of these nice girls like Zia, she is beautiful and you know she is my god daughter. I don't have to tell about her family. Their wealth matches ours."

"Well I'll think about it father" he told him to make him happy. But his thoughts were otherwise occupied with what his father said about his mother. Then Quinn's head jerked as though some one had kicked him at the back. So he still loved mother. Mr. Patterchinni never talked about his wife after her death. But before Quinn's mother died she had left them and gone back to England. Mr. Patterchinni had refused to talk with her till she died. Now Quinn understood. The old man had loved her but he vehemently refused to accept that because his pride had been hurt. But many years after her death, one day he told 'Perhaps she was home sick and I should have understood'. Quinn was happy in a way that his father was hurt and not angry with his dead mother for he loved his mother too. He was torn between two devotions. But he stood by his father. That was one of the reasons he did not want to get involved emotionally with anyone because he feared for a similar situation. There were times one or two affairs became serious, mostly from the other side but Quinn quickly made it clear that he was not ready to plunge into matrimony. In certain ways Quinn was a replica of his father.

'And now the old man wants me to settle down' a slow smile spread through his face. But who? Quinn closed his eyes wearily for a moment and to his surprise he saw the beautiful face of Valerie. It was a mental shock for him. Driving through the roads the bitter sweet memory of Valerie haunted him. And it was here on the lonely roads of Rome far away from Valerie he realised the truth that he had fallen in love for the first time in his life with a woman whose beauty and charm he could never forget. But how could he forget why he employed her in the first place.

Torn between two different kinds of emotion he reached the family Villa. The servant opened the door and asked with concern "How is Senior Patterchinni Quinn"?, he always took the liberty of calling his junior master by his name because he practically brought him up after their mother left them. "None the better but still there is hope" he answered in Italian. The servant nodded his head with understanding." Would you like your dinner to be served"?, it was a question of routine. " Well, not yet. But you can retire to bed Vichini, If I need anything I'll take them myself." Quinn dismissed him politely, and he walked straight to the cabinet and poured himself a strong drink. He took the drink and sat down in the study of the old man. He wanted a deviation from the present mood. Then he remembered the letter his father mentioned and he opened the safe and traced the envelope with the English lawyer's frank. Before he started to read he drank half of the drink in the glass, he needed it.

The letter was addressed to *"Dear Papa and Quinn"* dated and timed May 10th 11a.m

> *At last I have taken a decision and I want you to know that nobody is to be blamed for that except my fate. For a long time I hid the unhappy time I was having with Haward, thinking of the heart ache you had due to a similar situation when mother left us all. A year after Patricia was born I found out that Haward is not the man whom I believed to be. He had a lot of involvements with illegal activities with other countries but worst of all he was using women with whom he spent most of his time making the others believe that it was me his wife.*

She quoted various incidents with dates and the fights they had over it

> *I didn't want to make you unhappy by coming home. But it is too late. I am mentally distraught and I would be equally miserable if I leave my husband, so I have decided to take my own life. But I have given strict orders to Haward that he allows Patricia to live with you or I shall expose him to the world by asking my lawyers to send all the proof I have for his arrest. I have personally requested the lawyers to send this letter after three months from this date. If you receive this letter that means Haward had not given any trouble in allowing Patricia to come and live with you. If that has not happened at the time you receive this letter please use all these documents attached to this letter to give pressure to him to do so. I know what I am doing is not correct in the moral sense. But the truth is I still love Haward and can't live without him.*

I love you
Gina

Quinn was caught in an emotional tangle after reading the letter. He and Gina were attached to each other before she married and went away, and it gave him considerable amount of pain to know that she was no more. He stared at the book shelf for some time. 'So nobody forced her to take her life'. Suddenly it dawned to him that except Haward nobody was to be blamed for Gina's death. Then he realised that the report Valerie did had nothing to do with Gina's decision. Quickly he looked at the date of the letter again. 10th May that means two days before Valerie's report. Words could not express how he felt. Partly relieved, partly happy partly dismayed, on the whole it was more of a mixture of several emotions. At last the facts rebut the assertion and exuberant liveliness diffused leaving him with the feeling that he was free to fall in love with Valerie without any barriers what so ever. But is it enough'? Doesn't Valerie have a say? What if she doesn't love him? Now he was drawn into a new situation of anxiety. I should give some time to know her heart, and in the mean time I should clear some matters without hurting her. He was happy that he fell in love with her even before he knew that Valerie was not the cause for Gina's death as he believed all these days. He got up from the chair and went to his bed room. He sprawled on his bed thinking about Valerie, every detail of her and when he drifted to sleep he was kissing Valerie full in her mouth in his dreams.

Chapter 22

Valerie's Entry:

I feel I have not seen you for ages. But another voice within me says I may have to live without you in the future. I decided now it self I should be prepared for that. I am slowly building a fortress against the misery I may have to face one day. Every day when time permits I will say 'I love you for better or worse. and the word' worse" two times. At the office I looked round for something special, then I saw a group photo. When people were not around I took a photo in my mobile phone. It was not a clear photo but at least I could see you. This is my secret, to carry you where ever I go and to see you when ever I want. Even you can't stop.

"There on a shelf is a picture of you"

The next two days were uneventful for Valerie, except on Friday she received a call from Hans Hoffmann. When Miss Wagner said that Mr. Hoffmann was on line she was quite surprised but took the call. "Hi! Miss Wilson, I returned from Holland only this morning and Miss Roth told me you called. Would it be possible that we could negotiate the price sitting together, either in your office or in mine", he came to the point without any frills. He had more of an American accent Valerie noticed. "Mr. Hoffmann please don't mistake me for telling this, but I would prefer to talk anything official only in the presence, of Mr. Patterchinni. So I am afraid you have to wait for such an appointment when he is back in Berlin" she said cheerfully but firmly. "Well then how about the beginning of next week?" "It all depends when Mr. Patterchinni returns, Mr. Hoffmann", Valerie stressed. "Don't you have any means of contacting him and fix an appointment". He was a bit demanding. "I am afraid it is not possible because he had gone on a private visit and I prefer to wait till he calls Mr. Hoffmann". She was not prepared to face one of Quinn's moods calling him home." I see", he was hesitant," Well let me know as soon as possible. "There was a pause on the other side. Valerie was about to bring the conversation to an end when he suddenly asked, "Miss Wilson are you free this evening?" Valerie did not expect such a development. And she was not armed with an answer so she simply said, " Not to my knowledge." Hans took the lead. "Then would you mind coming out for dinner with a few of my friends tonight?", it was more of a plea. Valerie did not answer immediately. Interpreting the silence as an advantage he said" Well I will collect you at the office at Six O'clock. "Mr. Hoffmann you mistake me. I didn't say I will come." Valerie said losing her patience. "Miss Wilson I am not going to eat you, after all we are two grown up individuals and I promise you I won't talk business." Again Valerie was dumbfounded lacking a quick answer. And before she could talk he closed the conversation with "Okay. till six o'clock then, Bye" Valerie heard the click. With the receiver in the hand she was thinking what she should do. She was only casually dressed for one thing, and she had no special desire to go with him. She traced the telephone number and called Mr. Hoffmann's office. There was a lady who spoke in German. She gave her name and requested to speak with Mr. Hoffmann. She said she was sorry to say that Mr. Hoffmann had just left the office and would be back only the next day. It sounded like a routine answer. At first she thought to leave the office early and leave a message at the information desk with an excuse of a head ache. But then her rebellious nature argued I should rather face him straight than act like a coward for no reason. After all I am in a responsible position and I should be able handle situations like this, further more he said there will be others so it will not be an intimate party for two. And high time she met some people. Deciding on this she concentrated on the work she was doing. At quarter to six she got up and went to the ladies room to do her face and with a touch of lipstick she saw her reflection in the mirror. Satisfied with the results she took a small bottle of perfume and dabbed it behind her ears. At the back of her mind she was thinking, perhaps it was a chance to know this man before they meet officially to negotiate the contract. The advantages of the contract with his firm with a reasonable reduction will be the best out of the three. Having no regrets of making the decision to go out with Hans she came out of the room. Sharp at six she heard the buzz of the outer door and when Miss. Wagner opened the door, Hans Hoffman walked into the office handsome as ever with a bright smile, a plain looking woman and a thin man following him. Valerie went forward to meet him and he introduced the other pair as Mr. and Mrs Smith from The States. She shook hands with them and Hans said "Shall we make a move". Nodding her head she walked towards the door. Most of the staff had left the office but those who remained had a blank look except Miss. Wagner whose face showed a surprise which she was quick enough to hide. Outside at the car park, Valerie allowed the two men to take the front seat and took the rear seat with Mrs. Smith, an arrangement which was clearly not to Hans' pleasure. He looked at her through the corner of his eyes before he started the engine. Seeing her car, brought her the thought that she needed the car for the next day. She reflected this thought loudly and of course Hans heard it. "Don't worry if you don't mind I could pick you up at your place." It appeared to be an innocent offer. But Valerie did not like the idea of going with him to the office. Quickly inventing an excuse she said, "Thank you for the offer but I don't want to trouble you. Susana would collect me tomorrow." Hans' hands gripped the steering wheel and Valerie could see the tension behind that handsome face. Certainly she had chosen the wrong thing to say. For there was a silence, before he said, "Does Susana have a partner Miss. Wilson"? "Not to my knowledge" Valerie was determined not to discuss Susana's or any body's love affair with this man. "You know that we were engaged once", was there a kind of triumph in his voice "I am new to the office and I have various other things to do than digging other people's past Mr. Hoffmann." she said acidly. At this point Mrs. Smith intervened and asked "Do I know that young lady Hans"? "Not a chance Betty, We broke the engagement long before I met you and Roger" Betty looked awkward so she changed the topic by asking, "What kind of food we are having today Hans?" "It's typical German food, it is a restaurant owned by one of my partner. I thought it will be a change for you and Miss Wilson". This time he smiled and that made every body at ease. They were driving through the busy streets of Berlin and she was able to see an unusual amount of people heading towards the underground station. Unable to resist she asked " Is there a kind of festival today?" Hans was carefully avoiding the rush of traffic before he said "A kind of. Every two years we have the Consumer Electronics and Communications Exhibition for ten days at the International Congress Centre, one of the biggest in Europe. Almost all the companies represent themselves. Quite interesting." "Oh that should be quite exciting to visit." Valerie said with genuine interest." "Care to go?" that was the second time he offered. This time she could not ignore it. So she said "Well it depends on when" "Unfortunately it is from nine to six." " Quite an inconvenient time for me" Valerie was happy her reason sounded plausible. By now they have reached a quieter area. Valerie looked out and saw a lot of single houses than in other places. "What is this place called?" asked Roger who was a silent listener all these time. "We are speeding towards the area called Dhalem, most of the rich people live here. It is our Beverly Hills. You have never been to this area Miss Wilson? he asked slightly turning his head. "No" Valerie's answer was curt. The car turned to a side street and Hans said "Here we are." Valerie saw a very expensive looking restaurant not huge but big. Hans parked the car and Roger got out of the car and opened the rear door for the ladies, but Hans was quicker to come to the second door to open it. Valerie got out of the car and Hans led them all to the main entrance. Obviously Hans was recognised by the staff and the head waiter came and spoke in undertones with Hans and then nodding his head he showed a table for four with the card 'Reserved'. Once they were settled the head waiter was there with the menu card. Finishing the selection of wine he asked the others to choose the, food from the card. As every thing was in German language, Valerie needed help like the others, and looked helplessly at him. "Leave me to select for you Miss. Wilson so that you don't miss the delicious food of ours", Hans said politely. The meal was excellent and they exchanged polite conversations in between. Hans was a perfect host. It was towards the end of the meal that Hans suddenly asked. "What were you doing before you joined the QP enterprise Miss Wilson"? Valerie almost choked before she answered "I was the Production and Marketing manager with an occasional chance to do reports on the television." "How interesting" it was Betty who spoke now. "Do you think your present job is equally tempting"? Hans asked with a challenging glance. "Its more of a challenge, I should say. I always wanted to work in a foreign country and when I got the chance I took it that's all". Her direct smile convinced her words, although Valerie thought she saw a quick raised eye brow, on his face. "So you are not a personal friend of Mr. Patterchinni?" "Of course not! I was selected after I sent in my application." Valerie replied quickly. Did she see relief on his face. She was not sure. When the dessert was served it was close to mid night, and seeing Valerie's restlessness Hans said "Shall we..."? Valerie was the first one to rise from the chair. Coming out of the restaurant Hans asked, "By the way where do you live?" She told the address and he said, "Well it is closer to my place. Would you mind if I drop Roger and Betty at their hotel before I take you back home"? Valerie knew she was trapped. But she did not want to show him that she was frightened of that. It would look childish. So she said, "Of course not." This time when they got into the car Hans made Betty and Roger to take the back seat and Valerie had no other alternative other than to take the front seat. Except for an occasional question and answer they were silent through out the drive, and Valerie kept herself out of the conversation. Some how or the other Quinn occupied her thoughts. So when the car stopped at the hotel she simply blinked before she realised Betty and Roger were saying good night to her. Ashamed of her manners she bade them good night. Hans' car sped through the night. Noticing her silence Hans asked "Tired?" There was a kind of tenderness in his voice. "'Well a bit", she answered truthfully. "I hope we could do this often" he said. Valerie did not reply "Your thoughts are with your boy friend in England I suppose", was that an invitation for her to talk about her self? "No Mr. Hoffmann, I don't have a boy friend, if that answers your question" she said. He laughed so loud that she turned and looked at him. Hans said, "It is not healthy for you. Why don't you allow me to act like your boyfriend?" It was said in such a way that she couldn't get angry. Instead she said, "When I need it I will definitely let you know", they were silent for some time. Valerie drifted into her own thoughts when he said "Here we are" he stopped the car. Valerie thanked him for the dinner and walked towards the door. Hans stopped the engine and asked, "Don't I get a cup of coffee?" Valerie heard the warning bell ringing in her head. She answered firmly "Not to day Mr. Hoffmann, maybe some other time ", and continued to walk towards the entrance of her flat without looking back. Only after she reached the top of the stairs she heard Hans start the engine. Did he hope she would have second thoughts? Valerie was thoughtful when she inserted the key into the door. She heard the phone ringing. It took her a few seconds to reach the apparatus. But the moment she touched the receiver it stopped ringing. Who could that be? Father... Sally... Susana... She never dreamt that none of her guesses were correct. She couldn't do anything other than to sit and wait for the caller to call again. But the phone never rang, till she went to sleep.

Quinn could not give a reason for his anger. But he was angry. That was the third time he had called Valerie's number. He simply wanted to hear her voice. The more delayed the more eager he became. And the frustration made him to wonder all kinds of things including a suspicion that she might have gone out with a new boy friend. But his sensible mind said not to behave like a teenager with the first taste of love. It was a fight between reason vs. feeling. At last defeated by reason he decided to wait till next morning. He couldn't sleep so he thought how he should approach Valerie and find out her feelings. He was sure, she more than liked him, but was it enough for a long lasting relationship?' I should give her some time' he decided and took a strong drink and went to bed. For a long time he enjoyed Valerie's company in his dreams before he went into deep sleep.

Chapter 23

Valerie did not want to bother Susana or anybody else regarding a lift to the office. She thought of taking a taxi and called the number. She gave instructions to the driver about the address and the time and placed the receiver back. Soon it started to ring again. She lifted the receiver and said "Hello!". It was Hans.

"I forgot to ask whether you need a lift to the Office. If you want I will call you in half an hour's time, Miss Wilson"

"Thank you very much but I have made my own arrangement Mr. Hoffmann" she said.

"Were you angry last night?" the question was with full of tenderness.

"Of course not, I was only a bit tired" she tried to be normal.

"Then I could hope to have a drink with you one of these days". The enthusiasm he showed was obvious. "We will see" said Valerie laughing. He also laughed and called off. She replaced the receiver and turned to go when it rang for the second time. Thinking it was Hans again she said, "I have to leave for the office now."

"So early" said a voice which made her heart to jump.

"Hello" she said after a pause.

"Hello! A beautiful good Morning! "said Quinn.

"Good morning Mr. Patterchinni, I thought it was somebody else".

"Well I didn't know people called you so early in the morning. Some one important?".

"Oh no just a casual acquaintance. Is it anything urgent that you wanted to talk?" He wanted to shout and say,' Yes I love you Darling, and do you love me?'.

But he smiled to this idea and said, "It's just to call you and ask you about any new developments at the office during my absence "he hid his excitement in his voice with a laugh.

Valerie's own excitement was crushed by this inquiry so she said "In fact I wanted to call you and ask when you will be returning." There was a pause on the other end, and she continued "Mr. Hans Hoffmann would like to have an appointment with you to negotiate the price for his former offer. And if you could tell me a date I could confirm with his marketing manager." So she was not dying to see him. Quinn closed his eyes with a kind of unknown pain before he said "If every thing goes well I should be there in a few days time, and you can give the appointment for the end of the week." After a pause he added, " By the way I called you yesterday evening but you were not in the flat", he couldn't hide the disappointment. But for Valerie it sounded as though he was probing her privacy: She said ; "I went out with some of my friends for dinner, and returned quite late "Oh I see" He could well see that she did not want to say with whom she went. A pang of jealousy crept through his nerves.

"I suppose you enjoyed it very much "

"Well a change from the routine is always good."

"I didn't know that. May be I could also give you a change when I return" Valerie only laughed, The light hearted laugh on the other side made Valerie to think for a moment that she was talking to a young friend and not to her boss.

Quinn really wanted to talk some thing personal, so in a spur of a moment he asked

"Miss. Valerie, would you like me to bring some thing from Italy?", Valerie was shocked not because of the question but the way he said her first name. She could never think of an incident which brought them for an intimate situation. And now she was dazed and confused. So she said" Nothing in special Mr. Patterchinni except your safe arrival. "

Quinn felt a thrill over his body. So she cares and he said "You have a generous heart Miss. Valerie, I know very few people who share your wish". Valerie realised her courage for not showing her feelings to him was slowly retarding. A little more of this talk may lead to a situation she may later regret she thought.

Deciding to put an end to this she said "Soon my taxi will be arriving to take me to the office Mr. Patterchinni. " She gave him the signal. But Quinn was diverged into another direction now.

"What happened to your car?" he really was concerned.

This query broke Valerie's present mood and she said curtly "Nothing at all. Yesterday I got a lift and I had to leave the car at the office. That's all".

Quinn noticed the change in her voice. 'You fool, is this the time to show concern about the car'. "Never mind, I was only concerned about you, in case of an accident." He could not interpret the silence at the other end, so he said. " Let me not take your time. Have a nice day."

Valerie could not continue her silence and she said, "I wish you a nice day too Mr. Patterchinni." Both wanted to add the word 'darling' but both did it in their hearts.

Driving to the office in a taxi gave ample opportunity for Valerie to think about her recent conversation with her boss. How nice he sounded when he was away. The tenderness the caress and the concern he showed in his voice was quite disturbing. But will he be the same when she meets him in three days time? That she had to wait and see. She really enjoyed talking to him and now that it was over she wished she had continued with the conversation. What she suspected as love was confirmed now. This realization gave her a kind of feeling she never experienced before. The more she thought the more convincing it appeared. She was sure that the feeling she had for Quinn was certainly different from what she had for the advances shown by Hans Hoffmann. Shyness came over her when she thought about Quinn. But opposing instincts compelled her from going further into the analysis and blocked her train of thoughts. A red light blinked at the far corner of her heart. Like the titles of horror films it appeared as a small dot and became magnanimous. She clearly saw and shrank when it took the shape of an eight letter word 'Patricia´. The taxi jolted before the building complex and so were her thoughts. When she got out of the taxi she felt as though a string of pearls had fallen on the road and she had to pick them up one by one.

Valerie entered the office and saw Susanna already talking with

Jasmine. Her entry made both of them to look in her direction. The look that Susanna gave told her that already her dinner appointment of the previous day has reached her ears. She was not ready for a confrontation in her present mood. So she greeted them both with a 'Good morning Miss Klein! Good morning Mrs. Asadulla! 'remembering Susanna's advice about the behaviour at the office, and proceeded towards her room. Then remembering that, she had to collect her keys from Miss. Wagner she turned towards the information desk. The telephone at the desk rang and Miss Wagner receiving the call smiled and said, "She just came in Mr. Hoffmann" Her voice was one octave higher than usual, making sure all the people in the main office heard her, for they all turned and looked at her. Valerie quickly decided not to take the call and made a desperate sign to Miss. Wagner who in turn replied, "but at the moment she is busy talking with someone. Would you mind waiting on the line Mr. Hoffmann"? There was a small pause while she listened what was being told and then said, "Okay Mr. Hoffmann", and replaced the receiver. Valerie approached Miss Wagner and told her, "When and if he calls the next time tell him that the appointment he asked with Mr. Patterchinni will be this Friday any time in the morning" then thinking this will give him an excuse to call her in the pretext of asking for time, she added "or rather say at eleven." There was relief on Susana's face and Jasmine tried to go out of the room. Noticing that with a smile Valerie called Susanna and went to her room. Susana pulled one of the chairs and sat down with a sigh.

"Anything wrong?" asked Valerie with concern.

"On the contrary, Bob and I had a hectic time for the past two days as Mr. Patterchinni wanted Bob to take an executive post in Italy. And look Valerie what Bob has given to me" she stretched her left hand to show the diamond ring glittering on her hand. Valerie was really happy for the girl so she said, " congratulations! I am really happy Susana. Are you getting married soon?" Susana laughed and said, "It is true it was love at first sight for both of us. Bob wants it as soon as possible, but I have told him he has to wait till he takes over the new office in Italy." "Oh you

cheat! The way you said I thought you had asked him to wait for years."
Both of them laughed. Susana's blush was becoming of her and soon she
started to talk about her future plans. Both of them were engrossed with
their talk that it took a little while to notice that the telephone was
ringing. Valerie hesitated to take the receiver and motioned Susana who
was closer to the phone to take the call. "Susanna Klein" she said. Then
suddenly her face changed and covering the receiver with her hand she
said with a mouth movement "It is Mr. Patterchinni from Italy"

For a moment Valerie was lost for words and action. Slowly
recovering the shyness that came over her she took the receiver from
Susanna. "Hello! Valerie Wilson here", she said with a weak voice.

"Hello Valerie I just got the message that my father had a mild heart
attack and that means I had to extend my stay for a few days more. Could
you manage till I return to Berlin"?

"Of course Mr. Patterchinni, and I am sorry about your father", she
did not know what to say further. But Quinn on the other side said in an
impatient voice, "Well I am the only one he has now." Valerie
remembered what she heard about the sister's death and said
sympathetically, "I understand that Mr. Patterchinni, Please don't worry
about anything." There was some interruption and she was not sure what
he said. Then she heard him say "I will keep you informed. In case of
emergency you know where to reach me. I will call you this evening if
possible", there was a softness in his voice which she couldn't quite
understand. She only said "Yes Mr. Patterchinni and please keep me
informed about your father." "Yes of course, so till this evening" he
prolonged the pause for a few seconds and then added "Good bye". She
was still with a frown when she looked up and saw Susana looking at her
with a raised eyebrow. Valerie did not know whether to tell the whole
conversation or not. But Susana's face showed her that she had been
following the conversation for she said " I hope nothing terrible
happens" Valerie did not like discussing private things about the boss in
the office. Although her thoughts were with Quinn she turned towards
the phone as she said "I suppose I ought to call Mr. Hoffmann and

cancel the appointment". It was then that Susanna said "I hope you are not developing an attachment to Hans Valerie. Since I know him I had to warn you. He is not your type and he can hurt you as he did to me." When Valerie opened her mouth to protest Susana waved her hand and said, "Don't think I am jealous. I am extremely happy with Bob, It was love at first sight for both of us and I think we understand each other. But with Hans it is different. He can be nasty when he chooses to be selfish. At times not even an angel could bear him. I say this only to prevent you from getting hurt. Take it or leave it". As she said this Valerie could see a sadness come over Susanna's face which disappeared in a moment. Valerie knew that she has been really hurt. Valerie said, "If you mean that I get romantically involved, then don't worry. My relationship is purely official and so it will stay. Any way he is not my type Susana. And thank you for the warning. I will keep it mind". The other girl let out a sigh of relief. Then cheerfully said, "But I won't say the same thing about Mr. Patterchinni. He is any girl's dream" She winked her eyes and Valerie joined her in the laugh that followed. She called Miss Wagner and asked whether Mr. Hoffmann called and when she said no, she told her that she would call him and dialled Miss. Roth's number and told her what happened then in a very pleasing way told her she would let them know as soon as Mr. Patterchinni returns to Berlin. She was glad she did not talk with Hans. When she finished her conversation she saw that Susana was preparing to go. She also got up from her seat and shook hands with Susana and wished her again a happy future.

Valerie had a lot of work to do that day and she concentrated on her work. When she went to have a cup of tea her thoughts came back to Quinn. What would be he doing now? Perhaps he was at the hospital with his father or taken Patricia to visit his father. The second part of the thought made her a bit uncomfortable. Why was she feeling like that. For the first time in her life Valerie was curious to know about another woman which surprised her. Quinn filled her heart and soul. Though he was not physically present she felt his presence in every nook and corner. The yearning to be with him increased every minute. Many a times she was tempted to call him and shyness prevented her from doing so.

This realization also revealed the other side of the truth that her love would end up only in a bitter sweet memory. There were tears in her eyes. What was she expecting? Definitely not a security like a marriage. It sounded so low and temporal, compared to the pure beautiful love. She knew her love was beyond any boundaries and limitless.

Valerie's entry:

What a great delight when one of my wishes came true. You called me Valerie. How sweet the name sounded when you called. But at the same time the message you told me was not what I wanted. Hearing the voice itself is a treat for me. You simply caress me with your voice. I felt your hands stroking my head. I am sure it is not your habit to flirt with women. But why this special softness. May be the feeling is mutual, How I wish I am with you in Italy. Just to stroke that thick hair and look into those powerful eyes for ever, adoring every minute of it. I have a divine happiness. I am sure 1 will feel the same whether you love me or not.

'cos I'm not made of wood and I don't have a wooden heart'

Chapter 24

A few days went by without any news from Quinn. Her anxiety increased but she had no one to share with. At last she couldn't bear it any more. She tried his number only to be told by the automatic machine to leave a message. She dared not. Unfortunately she did not know where else to reach him. She was forced to wait. Only later she reflected if she had reached him what would have she told. She did not have anything that needed his immediate attention. May be she would have asked a trivial question regarding the project, and looked stupid in the eyes of Quinn. She thanked her stars that she was not able to reach him. She could not continue with the work. She was looking at the big clock counting the minutes and hours and rushed back to her flat. Relaxed in her bath for more than an hour, scrubbed her self till the skin shone and went to bed.

Valerie's entry:

> *It is simply a torture not to hear your voice. May be some kind of force is preparing me for the coming years. I was frightened for that loneliness. There are times you are alone in this world and it could be more painful than physical pain. You could never share or explain, you alone have to undergo that phase. I am in that condition. Quinn I don't know why but I wanted to shout and cry. For all this you don't even know that I love you. The other day I was sitting and drinking coffee with Susana, when Jasmine came and tried to read the coffee residue prediction, a Turkish superstition. She said " You have hurt someone in the past': I can't remember hurting any one Quinn. But may be it was a warning for the pain I undergo now. Quinn please come quickly, I only want to see you. I know strong vibrations could affect people.*

`I hope and I pray, that maybe some day, you are with me, in my little room'

The whole of next day Valerie felt uneasy and suddenly in the afternoon that pain started. She tried to bear it but it became severe and she came out of the room. Miss Wagner saw that something was wrong and rushed to her help. With great effort she half spoke and half signed. By that time the others were coming to help. They tried to lay her on the near by couch but when things did not improve one of them called the emergency service. Within an hour Valerie was rushed to the University Hospital. They diagnosed it was acute appendicitis. An injection was given to reduce her pain and she was taken to the operating theatre. She felt the sweet taste of morphine only for a second then she lost consciousness.

Someone was patting her cheeks and she opened her eyes slowly to find a smiling face of a nurse bending over her. Valerie was still drowsy but awake. Her right side felt stiff and numb. It took some time for her to realise that she was in the hospital. Turning her head she saw Susana with a worried face. Valerie tried to smile but failed in the action. Susana came near her pulled the chair and sat down." How do you feel?", she asked. Valerie felt weak to talk and the nurse told some thing rapidly in German and Susana nodded her head. Then bending her head, she said "They say it is better you rest now, with all the medicines you will feel sleepy. And tomorrow you have to get up and walk a little." Valerie nodded her head, still under the influence of the sedative. She turned her head and saw first the colours and then her focus was better to reveal a beautiful bunch of roses and she smiled. Her eyes brightened before she fell slowly into a trance and then into deep sleep. Susana tip topped and came out of the room closing the door softly behind her. Valerie slept between numbness, pain and nausea. Middle of the night she called the night nurse to give some thing to sleep. She was woken by rather a harsh voice" Aufstahen, Bitte", then may be the nurse realised Valerie was English and tried her English proudly by saying "Stand up please". Valerie was fully awake now, typical after effect of an operation. She was asked to sit in a near by chair so that a student nurse could make the bed. For the nurse it was a routine, for the patient it was painful and unpleasant. But most of them do that with a smile just to save their faces. Here in the hospital fussing in any form was not tolerated. She looked at her self. She was dressed in hospital garments. Valerie often thought there was no difference between a patient and a prisoner in this aspect. With her tongue in the cheek she slowly walked to the wash basin to brush her teeth. Her hand automatically went to the right side. By the time she finished brushing and the nurse helped with the sponging of the body, the bed was made. She started towards the bed only to be stopped by the nurse. She looked at her inquiringly. "You walk a little bit". Bringing an artificial smile on her face she did as she was instructed. It was a relief at last when she laid down on bed. The red disinfectant smeared the garment, but she was warned to keep the wound dry. She felt half naked with only a hospital night gown. So she pulled the sheet up to her neck. The patient next to her must have come days before her, because she was quite independent walking about with her Joop house coat, heavy makeup and a strong Gucci perfume. She looked at Valerie with a pathetic look but the smile Valerie expected never came. She knew that these conservative Germans are quite reserved. Any contact with a stranger was done with a reservation. Valerie turned to the other side and faced the door. The Surgeon entered with his interns and greeted her without much enthusiasm, just gave a pat on the right leg for Valerie to react with a pain. He was explaining the interns the case giving Valerie the feeling as though she was more of an exhibit than a person and one of them copying his senior, gave a blank smile and the whole crowd passed on to the next patient. Later the ward doctor, a better edition of the crowd before, made Valerie to sit down and asked her to 'Inspire' (breath in) and 'Expire' (breath out). Valerie wanted to shout 'I don't want to expire' but kept the humour to laugh on another day. At about 11 o'clock Susana and a few of the staff came to see her. The normal formalities. Valerie felt she missed some thing. Susana arranged her personal things in the cupboard, chattered for a while and went. At about five, visitors came to the other patient and the whole crowd went out leaving her alone. Valerie only had an instinct which she thought as her wish and that was the presence of Quinn. She knew it could not be possible.

Suddenly the door opened and there he was. Getting over the initial shock she gave a weak smile. He did not come very close, rather he stayed at the foot of the bed and gave a look minimising his pupil that went straight to her heart. Valerie blushed. Then he beamed with a smile. Was he making fun of her. No he was serious. " How do you feel"? His eyes never left her face. She could not understand what he was searching on her face. She was at his mercy. He never attempted to touch her. He was asking about this and that, and when Valerie asked about his father, he looked worried. Quinn on the other hand felt sorry for her, he wanted to take her in his arms but in this condition he feared he might frighten her. Somewhere within his heart a fire was put off. He asked about her comforts and bade 'good night' promising to get the telephone and the television facilities. He must have had some one influential, for within half an hour she was given the phone and the remote control. That night she lay awake for a long time thinking about her intuition.

Valerie had to stay for a week before she was discharged from the hospital. Somebody from the office came every day but not Quinn. The days at the hospital were dull as ever. Susanna and Bob came on the last day finished the formalities and took her to the flat. Susana offered to take her to her flat but Valerie politely refused. So they went to her flat and Susana and Bob stayed with her for some time and took their leave, telling Valerie to call at any time. Before taking the final leave Susana went down and collected the post for her which she kept on the near by table. Valerie thanked them and went directly to bed. Lying there she called her father and said she was back from the hospital and not to worry. She took a book and started to read just to kill the time. She turned casually and seeing the post she reached for them. One from Sally, another wishing her good health from Margaret and her father who were informed by Susana, and there was the last much bigger envelope. Her heart stopped. She could see Quinn's bold hand writing and she opened it carefully stroking his name behind. A beautiful get well card signed with' Loving greetings and warm welcome 'and simply 'Quinn'. This could mean something or nothing. But for Valerie it was something to treasure. Then she remembered she did not talk to her entry book. So she took the entry book and started to write.

Valerie's entry:

> *Very often I have intuition or telepathy or inkling or hunch or what ever they call it for things that are going to happen. Unfortunately it was not for the good things but also for the bad things. Therefore I don't pay much attention and mostly ignore them. But this urge to see you I really wished because I knew it will never come true and besides the thought gave me a pleasant feeling, just the right thing for my lonely heart. But the moment you appeared at the doorway I started to believe in my power, blinked away my tears and I thanked my stars. You stared at me with those powerful eyes and beamed with that charming smile. That smile becomes of you. Yes the next thing that I love is that quick smile in the least expected moment. And I was losing hope that there is anything, when your card arrived today. I don't know whether it is formal or personal for you but for me it is a sweet memory.*

'The over powering feeling, that you may suddenly appear'

Quinn could not work the whole day. When he was eight he came from school one day bubbling with the news of his victory in sports and he wanted to tell his wish to become a football star. But his nanny said his mother was not keeping well, and one should not express future plans when some one was ill in the house, therefore he had to wait but he simply ran and burst into the room and informed that to his mother despite the objection of the nanny. One week later when his mother left them for good and died in an accident his nanny blamed him. Afterwards he never repeated that. This might be superstition in the eyes of many, but it had a great impact on him. He never said any future plans which he really wished to come true when some one was ill. Most of the people have weaknesses in the most surprising branches. Quinn never told about his secret fear to any one but never dared to break it, especially if they were wishes he really wanted. Therefore Valerie had no reason to know for his silence. He could not talk to her while she was at the hospital. He did not want to rush things and he really wanted to know about Valerie's feelings before he could say anything. `Perhaps ', he thought `this was a blessing in disguise, to know her feelings before I expressed mine.´

The prediction of the future is unpredictable but people always preach others and when it comes to one self they are influenced by superstitions and fear. Some say and the others do not, that is the difference. Very few, feel good after breaking a mirror on the wedding day in England, or will continue to walk after seeing a black cat walking from the left side in Germany, or will continue a journey after seeing a single Hindu priest in India. The incidents may be different but the beliefs are the same. They all have something in common. A fear of losing something they treasure. Maybe a possession, maybe a relationship, or may be life itself. Quinn was no exception.

Chapter 25

It was the first day at the office for Valerie after two weeks on medical leave. All the people gave a warm welcome including a bunch of flowers. She thanked them all and after exchanging the formalities went to her room. There was no sign of Quinn in the office. She felt disappointed. She could not work. She felt as though he was her driving force. She heard him coming and entering his room but suppressed the yearning to run to him, instead she waited for his call. It never came. It appeared he was avoiding her. That pained. A voice whispered she was being unreasonable. She should not have any demand just because it was her wish.

An hour passed and she did not do any thing, then feeling guilty she switched on the computer, at the same time she heard the sweet sound of his buzzer, she did not answer immediately but took some time to compose herself before answering." Yes, Mr. Patterchinni" " Would you mind coming to my room". " Give me a minute".

It was rather a warm day. So she was not surprised to see him in his shirt sleeves pouring water to drink. He was quite formal making her feel she was there to do the job and none of that intimacy that existed a few weeks ago was visible. 'Well if that is what you want that is fine with me ' and she looked down on the papers and started to read without even thanking him for the services and the card. It was Quinn who started the conversation by asking "How are you feeling"? The caress in his question made her to look up. For some reason he was not looking at her. She felt ashamed for her childish behaviour. She saw that peculiar cynical tightening of the lips. She wanted to shout and say 'I am fine physically only my heart is wounded.' but instead she said rather in a flat voice. "Quite well, Mr. Patterchinni". The lack of interest in her voice was misinterpreted by Quinn. The next question stunned her. " Mr. Hoffman has been telephoning several times inquiring about you. Did he call you"?

" Not to my knowledge, May be he wanted that appointment he asked earlier". She was boiling within herself for Hans' behaviour. "Well from what I understood he was not in a hurry for the appointment. Otherwise he would have asked me when he knew I was here." He sounded annoyed. " Well I have no idea. It is only a few days acquaintance" " Are you sure"?. She got the devil. " If you have called me just to offend me on issues which are my private affairs, then I will leave now and come when you have, real work for me." She got up when he said "Well if that's what you feel I will not discuss your private affairs. Shall we continue from where we left. The sooner we finish the better". He became very formal. The rest of the day they only worked on the project. In fact he left the office without telling her. She went to the rest room and came back to find him gone.

Valerie's entry:

> *It was painful to sit with you and work with bent head. It was rather warm and I asked whether I could open the window. You only nodded your head. When I returned to my seat I saw you had pulled your shirt sleeves closer to the elbow. It was then that I saw the scar on your right hand, the hand I love. You must have seen the look on my face and followed the direction of my eyes I guessed, because I heard you saying " a punishment for childhood mischief" I didn't know how you knew the next question in my mind for you said "I fell down a tree'. I wonder whether our minds are in harmony. I thought we were back to our old footing until I found out you had gone without a word to me. May be I should not expect too much from life.*

`Quit playing games with my heart´

Days of routine life. Office work and home. Nothing special happened in both places. The occasional stares Quinn gave while working was a confusion rather than a pleasure. They must have had some power because she felt them at the back, she felt them on her face, she felt them when her head was bent, and she felt all over. A few times when she looked up he shifted his stares very cleverly. "Good Morning", and "Good bye" were the only private words they exchanged to each other. Once she was struggling, trying to explain something in German and Quinn smiled, enjoying her predicament without coming to her help.

One day it was quite warm. Being in her room gave confidence of any intrusion so she removed her Jacket of her suit and started to work. She was still in her room when the buzzer sounded. There were documents that Quinn had to sign, so she quickly collected them and slipped her jacket on and rushed to his room. Quinn was talking on the telephone in Italian and when he saw her he motioned her to sit down. She could not look at him so she pretended to look at the news papers on the table. She saw him placing the receiver down. Slowly she lifted her eyes and saw him staring at her. These stares had become a habit. Feeling a bit uncomfortable, she shifted her eyes to the near by flower pot. Then she heard him saying "Your thoughts seemed to be far away. Shall we begin or you need some time"? Was he trying to pry her heart.

She smiled without changing the focus and said," I was prepared long before you finished your conversation."

"Well that was my little niece, she is such a cute little girl" That was the first time he had ever talked about his family, and from the softness of his voice she understood he was very much attached to his niece. Before they could develop the conversation the telephone rang and this time it was Bob, for he said "Yes, Bob, I have the estimate in one of the files, give me a sec. he placed the receiver and got up from his seat. "Miss Wilson, I may need another half an hour to finish some work with Bob, could we start after that"? His apology was in his voice. "It's alright Mr. Patterchinni", she replied and got up from her seat. When she turned to go she heard him calling her, "Miss Wilson one moment please" he walked towards her and came very close to her, bent a little and pulled down a wrong fold of the cuff of her jacket and gave a pat to the arm with a smile and said " Now you can go". The tenderness and the care he showed was so touching, that she tilted her head to an angle and said equally expressively, "Thank You" and left the room with an unknown pleasant feeling.

Valerie's entry:

> *Today I was cutting the apple, the knife slipped and cut my finger. I tried to grab my hand bag for the tissue, and failed in the process, and all the contents fell down to the floor with a clutter. I didn't know under which pretext you were there, but you were there. You held my hand and asked me to press the wound with my finger. But suddenly your thumb came down and pressed my finger, and stayed there a little longer than necessary. I felt we were together in body and soul. Your face was rather close to mine. You were looking at my finger, but I was in a closer range to your face, almost touching mine. Suddenly you pulled your thumb and looked through the window. Was there a kind of guilt on your face. I wanted you to feel good and at the same time make you understand that I did not mind. You simply brushed off my 'Thank you' and went out of the room.*

`Warm and tender as he can be ´

Quinn was angry with himself. For the past few days he was irritated with every thing he did, although he did not want to accept it was this love he had for Valerie. He returned from Italy with full of hope only to find that first she was ill and then the constant calls from Hans Hoffmann. He suspected she had been encouraging Hans in his absence. He could not get a direct reply from her. Working alone with her in his room was the greatest strain for him, and taking his leave at the end of the day was really becoming difficult.

Valerie's entry:

Today you totally ignored me. That was really hard. What have I done to get such a punishment. Outside the office I had no friends and I was so happy with your relationship that I never felt I needed someone. Sitting in my flat and dreaming about you made me extremely happy. I never had such tranquillity. The bliss of writing these entries and imagining your presence was the most beautiful thing I have ever had. Some how or the other I feel you never leave me, not a single moment. I am living in my own fantasy world with no one except you and me. I think I may have to live for ever like this.

`Dream of you when I'm lonely, dream of you when I'm sad ´

Chapter 26

Quinn could not wait any longer to find out whether there was something between Valerie and Hans. The next day he asked Valerie to fix the appointment with Mr. Hoffmann, and looked at her face. He could not fathom her feelings when she phoned. She looked up and told the appointment was next day at ten in the morning. He asked her to prepare for the meeting, and told, she had to do the negotiations and he will only be a silent spectator. Valerie wanted to show him how efficient she was in her job, so she excused her self to prepare for the meeting. Quinn waited for her return but she never returned. He controlled his curiosity and went out telling Miss. Wagner he might not come back. When he neared the car he did not get into the car, he took the cigarette case from his breast pocket and pulled one cigarette. He was not a chain smoker. But when under pressure he permitted himself one.

Valerie's entry:

> *I hated the smell of cigarettes or pipes. For politeness sake I tolerate when my friends smoke. I was so sure that I would never fall in love with a man who smokes.*
>
> *I heard you leaving, but I did not come out. But again my heart was heavy not to see you. So I got up and looked through the window. I spotted you with your characteristic walk. I expected you would get into the car and drive away. Instead you pulled some thing from your breast pocket and only when you cupped your hand to the lighter I realised you were smoking a cigarette. You were looking up at the sky and blowing the smoke. The first reaction of shock slowly vanished as I tried to accept, no that's not correct, I accepted that I love you whether you smoke or not. You made me to give up my principle because the love that I have for you is stronger.*

*Nothing stopped me from loving you. I could live with this love even
without telling you. A kind of serenity has invaded my heart. I love you
Quinn in a very special way that you or others can never understand.*

'There are no strings upon this love of mine'

The next day Valerie was prepared for the meeting. Thinking it was a
formal affair she dressed herself to suit the occasion. Of course she took
some extra care on her appearance with a spare look of designer
minimalism, but in the scheme of feminine competition. The profound
silence was a little too long when she entered the office. Valerie felt than
saw. She ignored that and prepared the materials for the appointment.
She was almost ready when Quinn came, scarcely glancing in her
direction. He wore an immaculate suit, and looked handsome as ever. He
entered his room and took some documents and walked a little ahead of
her before he turned and asked "Shall we go?". His amused cynicism was
the last thing Valerie expected. She nodded her head and followed him.
He deliberately allowed her to walk ahead knowing very well at one point
or the other she had to stop and seek his help. The inevitable happened.
At the main entrance Valerie did not know where to turn, so she halted
and waited for Quinn to join. "Oh, I thought you know the way ", he
provoked her. "Well I don't" she replied calmly. Nowadays he never
looked into her eyes and talked. He turned left and pressed the button.
For the first time Valerie entered Hans Hoffmann's office. She saw Hans
coming towards them with a beaming smile and when he came near
enough he stretched his hand and greeted Valerie first, allowing his hand
to linger on her hand before he greeted Quinn. There was more of
professional courtesy than friendliness in that. Behind him came a short
lady in her thirties whom Valerie assumed Mrs. Roth, his Marketing
Manager, and greeted very softly but pleasantly. They were led into a
conference room, which was prepared for the meeting. There were two
more people who were introduced as Technical Directors. The seats were
arranged in such a way that Quinn and Valerie sat on one side and the

others on the opposite side. Formalities like drinks and coffee were served followed by artificial smiles and unwanted laughs hushed to reverend silence. Then Mrs. Roth started her presentation. At one point she said "Then your company requested our company to give the estimate for the contract". Here Valerie interrupted "Excuse me, we did not, but you wanted the contract". Eye brows were raised when she corrected "Yes we came to you". Hans was looking at Valerie with admiration, while Quinn was staring at his coffee cup. There were some technical matters discussed and Quinn spoke only when the occasion demanded. They reached to the point of deciding the price. Valerie said "We have another offer. Only when it is lower than that we could accept." "What is your last offer?". Mrs. Roth mentioned a sum that was more than double and Valerie simply said "We are sorry, the other offer was much cheaper than yours. Therefore we can't agree to that '" At this point Hans asked "Okay. What will be your suggestion"? For a fleeting second Valerie looked at Quinn before she quoted half the amount. There was a hush in the room. Hans closed his eyes for a moment and then wrote a sum on the note paper and pushed it towards her. Her request was 1.5 Million, and he wrote it as 1.45 Million. Without a word Valerie passed the note to Quinn. He nodded his head with hidden astonishment. He was dead sure this was a special concession for Valerie. But Valerie knew Hans wouldn't have agreed if there had been no profit for him. They lived in Germany and they knew the cost.

Hand shaking followed with the promise to sign the contract as soon as it was drawn. Quinn showed signs of impatience by non committed conversation. Valerie felt it was time to go, for Hans attentions were not to her taste. She looked at Quinn and nodded her head. They took their leave, and were escorted to the door by Hans and the others. Walking towards their office they were quiet. Then just before they entered the office Quinn said "So he is really prepared to have some sacrifices for your sake." Valerie's blood rushed to her head. How can he accuse her with a comment like that. He really needed a punishment '. She glared at him as though he was an alien in the eighteenth century spirit. Gritting her teeth she said "That is a malicious accusation" and opened the door before he could reply. She did not want the others to see her present condition so she walked straight to her room. Quinn really felt small. He went to his room and sat on his chair. He was silent and still. Slowly it dawned to him wanting and achieving didn't always go hand in hand. He wanted to expiate this jealousy. His hand stretched to the telephone and then on second thoughts he got up and went to Valerie's room. He knocked and before she could say 'come in' he entered the room. Valerie had scarcely any time to wipe her tears and looked at him with tear stained eyes. Quinn only said " I am sorry. I shouldn't have said that." Valerie did not respond. He took his handkerchief and gave it to her. She did not take it. Instead she simply allowed the tears to run down her cheeks. Quinn took a step only to be stopped by a startled retreat by Valerie. He had a presentiment any further advancement will end up disastrous. He said "Please forgive me", and left the room. He was angry with himself and he felt he needed a breath of fresh air. He simply opened the door and walked out without a backward glance. Once in the main office he pretended to look through the mail for a few minutes and left the office without a word to anyone. People did not question the comings and the goings of the boss. He went to the car park got into the car and drove away. He knew that those words were said in a dreadful bitterness of spirit.

With heaviness in heart Valerie stared through the window and looked at the sky. She felt love was rather a punishment than a pleasure. She wiped her face, took her sunglasses and came out. There were less people at the main office. She went to Miss. Wagner wearing her sunglasses and pleading a head ache, left the office. She had no idea Quinn was not there. Miss Wagner looked at her strangely but did not comment.

The first thing she felt was to go and cancel the whole deal. Then she analysed the implications. First it would be a big misunderstanding between the two companies. Secondly officially she had no right to do so. Thirdly it was a proof of her ability. It was no easy feat to pull off now.

She set herself resolutely to fight her rights. She drove through the long alley from the Branden Burger Tor to the Golden Angel and parked her car in one of the side roads. She took a long walk, saw the tourists attractions just to spend away the time. When she returned to her car, the orange rays of the sun were peeping through the trees indicating soon it would be dark. She got into the car and drove back to her flat. She was looking for a parking place when she saw the familiar car parked opposite her flat. Then she saw him.

Quinn walked to her car and stopped her. Valerie reversed her car and parked it by the side walk. She got down and walked towards him. Quinn did not talk anything but led her to the entrance and waited till she opened the main door. Once they were in, Valerie climbed the stairs without waiting for the lift. Quinn followed. When she entered the flat he entered and closed the door swiftly.

Then he thundered "Where the hell did you go? I was about to call the police." Valerie had a gushing desire to punch him on the face. She controlled her self. Instead she stared at him and retorted,

" I am not a teenager to be looked after by guardians".

"But you should understand I am responsible for your safety". Valerie got the devil. "Perpetrators cannot be protectors", she exploded. Quinn 's face was expressionless. Only his jaw lines were moving. Then he looked away and said, " I have already said I am sorry. What else do you want"?

Valerie became vociferous about the injustice " What would you expect from me if I had committed the same mistake"?, she was close to reproach.

"Well my desires are not yours. If somebody had done this to me, I would have merely thought he was either ignorant or jealous".

"But you are neither, what else should I think?" There was less bitterness in her voice. "Well shall we call it a truce and go out for a meal for the successful transaction." Quinn changed the subject. She knew he was avoiding an answer and to prolong this meaningless argument would only result in dangerous revelations. Meekly she opened the door eager to change the atmosphere. Once they were inside his car she looked at her reflection. A remake of the face would have been better. But she looked at Quinn's face quickly. He looked tired, with dishevelled hair. Both were in the same boat. When he turned involuntarily she looked ahead the street. Quinn smiled at the way she was looking ahead whereas she was measuring him all this time. 'Well no more provocation, one is more than enough for the day ". He parked the car in front of a small restaurant and got out. " The food here is very tasty I heard, and only selected people come here. I myself am coming for the first time." But Valerie's instinct told he wanted to avoid known places. Obviously the people showed the least interest and after selecting the table he said "This is one of the places where they serve good English food". So he had a reason. Once they got themselves seated and ordered the meal, things looked different. They exchanged bright nothings till the meal was served. She was limp and miserable but Quinn on the other hand seemed to be enjoying the meal, but the quantity he consumed was far too less for a man of his age. Was he also pretending, Valerie had no idea. He insisted on drinking coffee which was not her taste. "A habit from childhood" he said unasked. Did her doubt vibrate in his heart.

It was one of the most wonderful meals that Valerie had ever enjoyed. Quinn luxuriously stretched and yawned. She heard alcoholic ripples that lurked beneath. " How about a walk down the street?" Quinn's question brought her to this world. Her legs were begging after the long walk she already had. But nothing like a romantic evening walk at least on her side. She smiled and nodded her head. The lights were throwing shadows on the streets. They only walked round the corner, Valerie saw him looking down and walking 'unemotional as a mushroom'. They were only a foot apart but still did not touch each other. She wanted to hold his hand and lean on his shoulders but she suppressed her desires. Suppose he was a man who thought that personal relationships are a mode of sex, or what if he thought the word passion means nothing else to him other than sex. No it was far too dangerous, especially at the moment of weakness. For some mysterious reason her instinct warned her that was neither the time nor place to show any of her noble feelings.

A thorough understanding was essential, otherwise there was a risk of being humiliated. Then nothing could be repaired. Quinn on his side was wondering about the silence that hung between them. Before he asked her out he promised himself to behave honourably. He was reluctant to broach any delicate subject soon after the mending. That is where the word 'fate' enters in people's life. How true when they said 'the gods cannot help those who do not seize opportunities.

They reached the car in silence, and drove in silence. He was making some comments like the weather was cold rubbing his hands. Valerie was frightened to look at him and answer because they were very close to each other. Both were aware of the nearness. He missed her street which she warned him, he grinned and took a 'u' turn and drove back to her street. When he parked the car he jumped out of the car in pretence of opening the door but actually he was afraid something personal and intimate might be inevitable. Valerie opened the door and got down and shook hands, formally thanking him and allowing her hand to stay a little longer a gesture she never did with any other man. He got into his car she waved and he waved back before mingling with the rest of the crowded traffic. Valerie waited till the tail lights disappeared at the far corner.

Valerie's Entry:

The day's events were so contrasting I don't know whether to be happy or sad. It was good we patched up things between us before the day was over. But your behaviour was quite strange. Nothing hurts more than accused by your loved one. Do you know how much I love you Quinn. No, you will never know. Sometimes I have the feeling you are so close to me. Especially when you served the meal at the restaurant. I never went out with a man to have a meal with so much of love in my heart. It is a nice feeling to see to be cared. How much I wanted to hold your hands. But there was something in the air. I felt shy looking into your eyes. When you took the wrong road and grinned afterwards, for a moment I thought you did it on purpose but I was not sure. Both of us were pre occupied. I carry love, passion and all the feelings in my eyes. That's why I couldn't look at you when you turned. Very often I had wished people looked directly at me and talked to get the complete message. From today I can't look directly at you and talk. I know there is nothing worse than people avoiding looking at you. Quinn I am not going to look at the bleak future without you but I want to relish every single minute I am going to spend with you. Because beautiful memories will be mine and mine only. No one can steal them.

`I carried my love not in words but in my eyes´

Chapter 27

The next few days, with the approaching Autumn, the weather was cold and windy and especially the absence of Quinn at the office gave a dull effect on the whole. Valerie wished he had informed her about his departure. She was informed Quinn had gone to London. She wondered why he evaded telling her about his departure after such an intimate evening together. Well may be he just wanted to make his amends for his mistake and nothing more. She felt the more she loved him, the less his attention was.

Quinn was, in his London office negotiating with Haward for Patricia's future, for he heard from reliable sources that Haward was planning to move to Hollywood. He couldn't talk about that with Valerie thinking he might be deprived of that display of intimacy he had gained. He realised that love was like a glass. It breaks when you are uncertain or hold it tight. He very much wanted to call Valerie, but what mitigation he would give. He preferred to be reticent than to lie. Truth might hurt her, if revealed in the most ingenious way. He was not yet sure of her feelings. He was not sure whether she had a soft corner for any body else. He was not sure of anything. He was sure only about his feelings. But that was not enough to develop a relationship. It was too early for anything. He had to wait.

As for Valerie she spent most of her time in her own company. In a spur of the moment she visited the project site. People were polite but she could sense opposition if not open hostility. She was prudent enough to ignore and show a false front by smiling at them. She came home with a tired heart than body. How difficult to live in this world!

The weekend came and went and still no news from Quinn. It was the middle of the week, and Valerie wanted to buy something at the city centre, so she drove to Potsdammer Platz. She was at the `Arcaden´

buying some cream at the Douglas when she saw Hans with a very beautiful girl. Valerie hesitated whether to greet him or not. Then he turned and saw her "Hello Miss. Wilson, are you alone". His eyes were searching.

"Yes Mr. Hoffmann."

"Would you mind joining me for a cup of coffee, we are about to go to Starbucks." She couldn't refuse the offer because she herself wanted to go there.

"Oh thank you, I really need something to drink." She replied honestly. He did not bother to introduce the lady who obviously had no interest to be introduced. Valerie was in a dilemma whether to greet her or not and at the end she chose to be polite and said "Hello". The girl smiled and said "Hello". Hans must have seen Valerie's confusion for he said " I am sorry, this is my sister Sabina, Sabina this is Miss. Wilson from London and I have business transactions with her company." She only smiled. But her smile did not reach her eyes. Was there hostility in those eyes too. Valerie was not sure.

They moved towards the tea house. When they settled themselves Hans went to the counter to pay and collected the tea for them. Sabina did not show any interest to continue a conversation. So when Hans came back they were still silent. "Well Miss Wilson how is life"?

Spontaneously Valerie replied " Quite dull, may be the whether.".

" But once you start with the productions, I am sure you will be quite busy. By the way your contract is almost finished. You might receive it in a few days time."

"That will be nice, though Mr. Patterchinni is not in Berlin at the moment" She volunteered and realising her mistake bit her tongue.

Hans' eyes met hers only for a moment and he did the most unexpected thing. He turned to his sister and said, " Sabina if you have some more shopping to do you could continue we will wait here." Valerie intervened and said " No, no I had to leave in ten minutes Mr. Hoffman, You please continue with your shopping." She observed his sister hated her at that very moment. Walking back to the car Valerie was thinking how strange people could love a person and hate a person on the first glance. Some men are out to use the first opportunity, regardless the consequence, and sure Hans was one of them. She apprehended the difference between Hans the seducer and Quinn the charmer. She rather appreciated the distance and subtleness in Quinn. She was comparing both of them for no apparent reason. And Quinn's reaction two days ago was confusing. Was that professional jealousy or private.' If it was the latter then I am fortunate" she wished.

****

Quinn needed more time than he anticipated for the transactions with Haward, and the two men did most of them by phone and only the signing was done at his office. Quinn was formal and showed none of that intimacy they had before. Once he called Valerie but was told she had gone to the project site. Although he finished his work on Friday he delayed his journey because he knew he could not see Valerie during the weekend. It was too dangerous to visit her in her flat after last week's incident. He was becoming quite possessive of her. Suppose things did not happen to his expectations then it would be humiliation, he reflected, especially with Gina's affair. With these things in mind he took the late flight on Sunday.

He arrived punctually at the office the next day only to find Valerie was not there. He stood near the window and looked down at the parking place. He saw Han's car entering. The green eyed monster kicked at him bringing hatred at the sight of Hans. Then he saw Valerie's car, and noticed Hans' hesitation. Hans went to the car and opened it and Valerie was greeting him. For reasons unknown his blood was boiling. Both Hans and Valerie were walking together towards the main entrance. He watched them till they disappeared. What is she trying to do? Playing a double game. He sat on his seat and spoke through the intercom "Miss Wagner, I am very busy, No calls and no entries." "Yes Mr. Patterchinni".

Valerie was helpless when Hans came and opened the door of the car. She tried to be polite and greeted him. But when he walked with her to the entrance she had an instinct that some thing was going to happen. She excused herself as quickly as possible by saying she had forgotten something in the car, in order to avoid going with him in the same lift. She was sure that will not give a good impression if her colleagues saw her. Therefore it took more time for her to reach the office. Quinn heard her coming and automatically looked at his watch. "Well surely she must have had a long chat with him ' he thought. The yearning he had in London sublimed and irritation replaced that. He tried to shut the thought of Valerie by concentrating on his work piled at his desk. He went through the letters and one of them drew his attention. It was from Hans' company. Quickly he opened to see the contract. Going through the contract he understood why Hans had agreed to such a low price. Hans was able to compensate the loss by the services he offered which were important but not discussed in detail. He smiled but did not want Valerie to know Hans cunningness. Hours passed and Quinn came out of his room in order to escape from the present depressive mood. Sleekly he looked in the direction of Valerie's room. It was ajar. To go or not to go that was the problem. He walked towards her door. Then changed his mind and walked to his room. He seated himself and in the intercom called Valerie. " Miss Wilson would you come to my room for a moment please." " Yes Mr. Patterchinni", she was quite formal. Regardless how much she loved him, she could not go beyond a certain limit to show that, especially when he was so distant that he did not have the courtesy even to say 'Hello' on his arrival. She came out of the room, her legs were stiff by sitting for a long time. She smiled at Miss. Wagner, passed her desk and entered Quinn's room. " Sit down Miss Wilson, We have received Mr. Hoffmann's contract. Read through it and when it is to your satisfaction then I will sign it.". He did not look at her. He was back to his past habit of talking to her with downcast eyes. In fact she was so used to that she allowed her feelings freely flow from her eyes. And suddenly he looked up. The pain in his eyes nearly killed her. Valerie did not know the reason. The contract was accepted by him then why should he feel sad about that. There was something wrong. But what? She tried to be cheerful and said" Now we could start the project". He was not that enthusiastic when he replied," I hope so". Surely there was something wrong.

Quinn wanted to point out the flaws in the contract and discuss them. But seeing Valerie's fervour to work on the project, thinking `may be she wants to work closely with Hans´ and misinterpreting Valerie's exuberance as her wish he simply said, " Well I could send it today itself for you to start working at the earliest". Valerie was vexed at the rate he was pushing her to work with Hans. Well it was clear he was not interested in her love and affection, when he had the love and devotion of Patricia. May be he felt Valerie more of an embarrassing encumbrance than any thing else and he wanted to push her away, so that he need not see her and eventually could get rid of her. All his previous anger was only to show her, first the job and then the rest. What a fool she was even to think there was a soft corner for her in Quinn's heart. He was only being polite. Well now the message was clear. She would be careful. When she looked up and spoke, her eyes were blank void of love, passion and all such feelings. She got up and simply said " Please let me know when I should start the work", and left the room without a backward glance. But she knew that this acting was possible only for a tenth of a second.

Valerie's entry:

Sometimes we think certain things don't leave us and we don't realise the loss till suddenly one fine day we miss it. As for me I miss it Quinn. I miss you, now that I know I am slowly losing you. I think my fantasies rode well ahead of time and I went with that wishing them to be true. I read a lot. Nothing in the form of literature escaped my eyes. Stories are truths and wishes of the authors. Only thing is one could not see which is what. So the tendency is, one is mistaken as the other. The result is wishes become the truth for me. But today you have woken me up from this illusion. But what about my love. Was it an illusion, No Quinn regardless what your feelings are, my love is pure, and the bitter sweet memories will always stay in my heart because I had to live with that.

`I'm bound to stay single till the rest of my life´

Chapter 28

Few days passed, and then things started to happen. Hans was in and out of the office, and whenever he came he was taken to Valerie's room and she worked sincerely and the day came when she had to go and inspect Hans' studio. Quinn was at the office only for an hour or two and very often when she most wanted him she was told he was out. She visited the site with Hans and organised every thing. Every day when she returned to her flat she was so exhausted she went to sleep as soon as her head touched the pillow. The production was coming to shape and she wanted to share with someone but she could not catch Quinn. At the end she wrote a note to him and left it on his table. The next day she was getting ready to go to the office when she heard the telephone ringing.

" Hello"

" Good Morning", Quinn caressed her.

Slowly she said " Morning".

"I saw your note", he continued " anything wrong?".

" No, I should know the proposed date of launching", after a pause she added "because we need to do a testing before that date"

"Well I will be at the office today, then we can fix every thing". She wanted to talk with him but words refused to come. It was the same every time she heard his voice. She could deliver a talk without any prior notice, she could report on the TV without any problem, and talk with anyone, anytime and anywhere without fumbling for words, but with Quinn it was different. She simply lost her articulation itself. Taking her silence as the sign for the end of the conversation, Quinn said " Okay. see you " and before she could say anything she heard the long beep of the telephone indicating the call had ended.

Valerie got ready and went to the office punctually, only to be told that Quinn would come only after twelve. Having nothing to do in the meantime she came to the outer office in pretence of making a cup of tea. She was about to turn when the door opened suddenly and Quinn appeared. Her brain refused to think, her muscles refused to move and her heart stopped for a moment. He looked at her, narrowing his eyes. She averted his eye contact fearing he would see the yearning she had and looked through the window. " Miss Wilson when you finish your tea you could come to my room". He did not stop but continued to walk towards his room. Valerie did not gulp her tea but sipped it taking more time than necessary, went to her room collected some documents and returned to Quinn's room.

Quinn purposely stood facing the cabinets so that he could see her in a better light but he was in the dark. Valerie was uncertain whether to sit or stand. Then placing the documents on the table she turned to Quinn who quickly busied himself with the papers from the cabinets. "Yes Miss Wilson, What is it you want?", he was quite casual. " I want you to go through these papers and tell me whether the plans are to your satisfaction. You should also give the dates in which you are available to watch the testing". She turned to go and found herself facing Quinn directly into the eyes. The sudden nearness brought a blush on her face and the grin on Quinn's face showed he enjoyed it. Then he did the most unexpected thing. He simply flirted with his eyes. The impact was tremendous and Valerie stumbled one step and his hands came to her rescue. The contact was electrifying. Valerie never thought till that moment that being in love could be so wonderful. " What are you trying to do? Why are you doing this to me?" he hissed. She looked at him with a pathetic look.

Suddenly the telephone rang and broke the spell. Sometimes such calls are ill timed. This was surely one of them. Taking the receiver Quinn said "Hello." Then his face changed. All the sheepish look vanished and he answered "Yes, she is here" he turned and gave the receiver to her without telling who it was. She held the receiver and she could hear Hans' voice. She slowly turned her head and looked at Quinn, he quickly turned and walked out of the room.

Helplessly she said " Hello Mr. Hoffmann"

" Hi Valerie this is Hans I just wanted to know whether you are free this evening to take you to a special restaurant. "

Valerie was so angry with him for breaking that wonderful moment she had waited, she rebuked him by saying ", I am sorry I already have a dinner date tonight".

" Never mind perhaps another time".

Valerie quickly added " Any way thank you for the invitation".

" It's a pleasure".

The call ended and Valerie came out of the room to see Quinn talking with one of the employees ignoring her totally. She turned towards her room when she was called by Quinn. He said in a passive voice " If you could tell me when the testing date is, I could watch where ever I am Miss Wilson. I think I don't have to be present at the office for that " He continued his conversation as though she had interrupted him at the most unwanted moment. Broken in heart Valerie answered to his back " Yes Mr. Patterchinni."

She did not see him anymore that day.

Valerie's entry:

After many months I cried bitterly today. Whenever I thought wonderful things were happening I was proved wrong. Those expectations, those dreams those wishes are so sweet that I live with them. But every time there is a mishap. Sometimes I wonder whether I have no luck in love. Quinn once and only once I want to hear that you love me. My flesh is strong but my soul is weak. I am simply crushed. How I longed that you talk to me in that soft caressing voice. I am a very shy person as far as personal relationships are concerned. But people never guess that. Quinn my love, I love you and I will never be able to get over this. No therapy could cure this sickness. Today I really hated Hans for shattering the most beautiful moments. But Why did your mood change Quinn. Do I believe in a false hope? I am going to write all my feelings in a letter especially my answers

to your questions, and post it to you that's the only way. May be you will
think I am a coward. But I don't see any other way.

`Gold and silver have I none, I can give you love´

The whole night she spent writing a real love letter though first time it was. The next day she called Miss Wagner and excused herself under the pretext of fever and begged her not to send any calls home. She did not want to work with Hans. Since they started to work together, Hans tried to be familiar with her. The whole morning she was feeling uneasy and often glanced at the telephone but it never rang. In the afternoon she took the letter and posted it with shaking hands. When she opened the door of her flat she heard the phone ringing. Slowly she approached the apparatus and hesitated for a moment before lifting the receiver.

"Hello", she said weakly.

" Hello", said Susana, "What happened?", she was really concerned.

"Just fever, I think I will be alright in a day or two". She told a white lie.

"Do you need any help"?

"No, no thank you, and when did you come back to Berlin?".

"Yesterday Evening. Bob is going to Italy together with the boss and I am visiting my parents in Potsdamm for a few days. If you really need me I will drop in this evening".

The news she casually said was like a blow to Valerie. She started to believe in fate playing a role in her life. Why he may not even read the letter for another week while she sat here lonely and blue. She wanted to ask when Quinn was going but something prevented her.

Instead she said " That was nice of you, But really I don't need any help, I hope I will be alright tomorrow".

When the conversation finished Valerie felt a funny feeling in her stomach. Was she hasty in writing the letter? What if he laughed at her? She sat down on the sofa and analysed her feelings. The fear she had at the beginning slowly evaporated and a kind of serenity settled with a light feeling in the heart as though a long carried burden was at last gone. Gradually she breathed the incense of ardour, passion, and fire of love. She never felt guilty but was happy that soon she would know how Quinn felt one way or the other. It was strange that both a positive and the negative answer would not tilt her in any way. Naturally she wished that he loved her. But if not, at least now she knew what was falling in love. And she was prepared to take any answer. One should not put the blame on others just because things did not work out as we wished. But pleasant wishes always brought sweet memories. She was sure she could live with them. Now she knew that Quinn was her first real love and the thought itself was beautiful. Naturally the waiting was not easy to handle. Neither staying at home did help her. She was not in a mood to have an empty talk with anyone. She read her entries and enjoyed them. She took the one and the only card that she received from Quinn and the card he attached to the flowers sent on her first day, put them inside the entry book, after caressing them a few times.

At six o'clock she switched on the television to watch the local news. Quinn was on the news! He gave a short interview about his new transmission. He looked both tired and moody. There were questions about his future in Hollywood for which he avoided an answer. Slowly the background came into focus and to her surprise she found it was the Tegel Airport in Berlin. So he was going away from Berlin and he would never read her letter till he came back. What kind of painful waiting she was going to have. The pictures changed to some other theme and Valerie allowed the programme to continue while she herself was not watching it any more. She bent her head backwards on the sofa and stared at the ceiling. She experienced panic, fear, yearning, passion and when she slowly closed her eyes, she only felt love, deep love descend upon her. Never in her life had the feeling of love violated her peace of mind like this. A change that never existed before spread over her, and her whole body shook a little, kindling the fire of love, and then again the fear of losing brought a few drops of tears. That feeling of insecurity was not a pleasant thing to have. It was like loosing foot in the swimming pool and breathing water instead of air, giving a choking feeling. Once the initial emotions sizzled off, there was serenity in her soul. In the stillness of her thoughts there emerged the beautiful truth. Whether Quinn loved her or not she could never stop loving him. Her tears were replaced by a mild smile slowly reaching her eyes, making them to open with a dream look that any man seeing that would have kissed them.

Chapter 29

She did not know when she went to sleep but middle of the night she suddenly woke up to see the TV still on. Automatically her hand stretched out for the remote control and pressed the stop button. The room became dark and she leaned on the sofa stretched herself and started the second part of her sleep. Next morning when she tried to move she felt her whole body numb and it took some time for her to get up from the sofa. She dragged herself to the bath room. There was no enthusiasm to go to the office with Quinn out of town. Staying like a coward at home was not going to help her in any way. She called the office to say she would be coming an hour later to the office. Well she need not worry till Quinn was back. She spent the least time in getting ready. The zealous sprit with which she got ready all these days was gone to the zero level. With the minimum of interest, minimum of glamour and minimum of anticipation she got into her car and drove to the office. The stoop she had with the drooping shoulders, the empty look in those otherwise beautiful eyes, the drag in her walk and above all a kind of black hole feeling in the heart were signs when you know the impossibility of meeting your loved one. Love gave a tingling effect on the body, great excitement in the heart, anxiety in the brain, sweetness in the memory, an uplift in the environment, happiness in the dreams, wakefulness in the sleep, fullness in hunger, delight in waiting and all in all love in loving.

When she reached the office she saw Quinn's parking place was empty. Instead Bob's Sports car was there. May be Susana had popped in she thought. On the corridor she met some of the QP Enterprise minor employees who either nodded or greeted with a "Morgen", more of a habit than manners. Valerie hated that mode of greeting without feeling. She had a puppet smile on her face. She longed to enter the office, go to her room and shut herself without facing any of those thoroughly artificial gestures. She opened the door with a bent head in order to avoid further of those comportments. Then she saw the most unexpected. The familiar shoes and trousers! Her eyes slowly rose to see Quinn standing at the reception going through the letters. A peculiar sound came from her, and Quinn looked up, smiled at her, grasped the rest of the letters and greeted her "Good Morning! And how are you?" The shock of seeing him made her to stare at him which confused Quinn, and then the slow shy smile replaced her face when she replied "Good Morning! I am better." Unaware, her eyes went to the bundle of letters in his hand. "Yes quite a lot after yesterday's interview I suppose" he said. Valerie understood he had not seen her letter. "Yesterday I went to meet one of my friends at the airport and the media caught me. The result is this", he showed the bundle. Valerie nodded her head with a half open mouth. " I am on my way to the airport, " he explained " I wanted something at the office so we had a short break " Then she saw who the `we' were. Bob was emerging from the next room. "Oh I see ", she said thoughtfully." I will be back in a few days, and then we could discuss those dates." Was he trying to apologise for his behaviour two days ago. Valerie automatically said, "Yes Mr. Patterchinni", and added to her self 'may be not'. It was too late to do anything. He has got her letter and there was no point in fretting over that now. Bob said " Hello", and Quinn's attention was drawn by somebody else while Valerie walked to her room. But before she opened her room she looked back more of an instinct than curiosity to find Quinn looking at her quizzically. Was there a message in his look. It was only a fraction of a second and then Bob took his bag and walked towards the door followed by Quinn.

For the first hour Valerie lost all her power and motivation to proceed with the normal tasks. She realised expressing her feelings in writing was easier but waiting for the result required tremendous effort. The possibility of hundred and one impossibilities, popped up and broke like a boiling liquid. What if he mocked?, What if he laughed?, What if he revealed to others?, And what if he refused? The last was the most painful. At last she came out of those thoughts and saw only one clear serene picture. Quinn filled her heart and soul. Though he was not physically present she felt him every where. And the long dwindled answer dawned. The love she had for Quinn was never ending and she would be happy to live with his memory if the worst happened. And a voice within peeped and said, 'Nothing wonderful had happen to me before and I am sure it never will. I will love him for better or worse', she repeated the latter part as a sacred vow. Nobody would believe such love existed in the modern times. The elder generation would call it unwise and the younger generation would say madness because they had never tasted this kind of love. For them love is passion before the union, passion and sex after the union and passion, sex, and devotion long after the union and they die with those three dimensions. But there was something beyond the normal love something unique, something wonderful, something out of this world and that was the love she had for him. Sure there would be times for secret tears you would have to endure, and secret joy you would relish but the love will be everlasting whether Quinn accepted or rejected.

Once her perturbation became crystal clear she was able to come out of her discomfort and concentrate on her work. Seeing the files on her table her conscience pricked. After all she was paid to do this job. She concentrated on her work giving a temporary halt for her love. When she went to have a cup of tea her thoughts came back to Quinn. What would he be doing? Perhaps he was in the hospital with his father or taken Patricia for a visit. The second part of her thought brought a slight pain in her heart. The yearning to hear his voice increased every minute. She was really tempted to call him but shyness prevented her from doing so.

It was shortly before closing time, there was a knock on the door. She said "Come in". Susana walked in with a beaming smile. Valerie stretched her hand to greet her and the sudden jerk disturbed the neatly arranged files and one after the other they fell on the floor and Valerie sat on her knees to fetch them. Susana was about to do the same when the telephone rang. Valerie signed Susana to receive the call. "Susana Klein" she said. Then suddenly her face changed and covering the receiver with her hand, she said " It's the Boss from Italy." For a moment Valerie was lost for words and action. Hiding her emotions and panic she took the receiver from Susana and said " Hello Valerie Wilson here." Her voice sounded feeble and weak." Hello Valerie, I had to extend my stay for a few more days. Could you wait for the test transmission till I return to Berlin?" "Of course Mr. Patterchinni, and I am sorry about your father" she added hastily. She did not know what to say further. She heard him mutter something like ' I wish you were here with me'. But there was some kind of interruption and she was not sure what he said. Then she heard him say " I will call you this evening, don't go out with anyone." There was a plea in his voice which she couldn't quite place. She only said "Yes, Mr. Patterchinni."

"Till this evening, Good Bye." Did she hear the word 'darling' or was it her imagination. She was still with the frown when she looked up and saw Susana looking at her inquiringly. Valerie did not know what to say.

But Susana's face showed her that she had followed the conversation for she said, " I hope nothing happens to the old man. Mr. Patterchinni is very much attached to him. And especially with one tragedy in the family not long ago".

Valerie wanted to know more about that but she was reluctant.

"He did not say anything about his father. May be some other reason. Did Bob call you"?

"Yes, as soon as he reached, that was two hours ago. I am sure he would have called if there was anything." She took her mobile phone and dialled. Valerie did not want to hear what was meant as private conversation, so she went out of the room in spite of Susana's protests. Within minutes Susana's head came out of the door and called her "Valerie come in. Bob says nothing serious had happened, except Mr. Patterchinni looked thoughtful. May be some family problem says Bob. Mr. Patterchinni is not with Bob right now. Therefore he has no idea."

Valerie wondered. She knew Quinn was not a person to get upset over trivial things. But he definitely sounded a bit excited or was it annoyance. Any way the fact remained she could not see him for some more days. Either he wanted to ignore her letter or he had not seen it and at the end of the day the pain was only for her.

Susana left the office after talking to her for half an hour. Valerie had a lot to do that day and she tried to concentrate on her work but without success. She went out to have a cup of tea but her thoughts were with Quinn. 'Perhaps he had not read my letter. Perhaps he was at the hospital with his father or taken Patricia to his father. Perhaps as Bob said there might have been some family problems. She tried to come out of the thoughts. But she felt, though Quinn was not physically present she felt him hovering around.

An hour passed and she was on the verge of accepting her instinct that was present from the beginning that she had to live with her dreams for ever. And that's all. This realization brought tears in her eyes and she was wiping them with the back of her hand when the telephone rang. Thinking it must be from Hans' office, she took a few seconds to control herself before she lifted the receiver." Hello " she said in a clipped voice. There was an intake of breath before she heard "Valerie" on the other side. Her hand shook, her lips trembled and her heart came to a stand still for a moment and her voice was so weak that it could be scarcely heard. Quinn on the other side thought that Valerie was not her normal self and he became panicky and asked "Valerie are you alright?"

"Yes", she answered in mono syllable.

"Is there any one in the room with you?" again she was able to answer only "No."

"Are you upset over something?" the third question brought her down to the earth. Quickly she said, " I am only surprised that you should call me twice within an hour."

"Could you guess the reason?" he caressed her with his hoarse voice. When he did not get an answer he point blankly said " I read your letter". Valerie let out a sound between hiccup and a cry.

"I am a very sick man to day Valerie. If I don't talk now I will become mad. Do you know the moment I knew about my sickness I couldn't sleep eat or drink!" Valerie really got upset this time. Not knowing how to take that remark she asked" Is there any thing I could do Mr... before she could finish he said "Please don't say that again. I will continue only when you promise to call me Quinn"

Valerie's heart sang.' For the past few hours no other name I was thinking', she mused. " Yes Qu...". Shyness prevented her from saying it further. The laugh Quinn gave at the other end was his success on winning her than anything else.

"Do you want to know why I called you today. It is not to inform you that my father is ill because it happened a few days ago and now he is recovering. "he paused to take a breath then he continued. "I wanted to tell this when you are alone so that I could have you all to myself. When I heard Susana's voice, I thought I would wait till she was out of your room. But believe me I had never wished a person to leave a place as I wished today".

There was another pause then he said, "Valerie Darling I love you". Words could not explain the various feelings Valerie under went at that moment. Her emotional response was unfathomable. She could not move leave alone speak.

" Valerie are you still there my darling?. Wouldn't you speak with me my love?" Quinn's begging was uncharacteristic for a man of his age and status. But if one knows the truth of love, 'love has no shame', then they would understand Quinn's reactions. He had lost two women in his life, his mother and sister before he could show them how much he loved them. And Quinn was not prepared to lose this beautiful angel before it was too late.

"Valerie darling can't you say some thing to me. Your silence is almost killing me" the passion and sincerity in his voice forced Valerie to speak.

"Quinn", she pronounced the name rather shyly," it is a pleasant surprise and I am dazed with that. Because today I realised that my love was hopeless".

"But why my darling?" This time he did not hide his excitement. "I thought you are otherwise fixed to another girl in Italy"

"Another girl? but who"? This time he showed surprise. Valerie uttered, "Patricia".

"Patricia?" He repeated the name, and then he started to laugh and Valerie blinked. Quinn realized he can't explain all the things on the phone. And especially he planned to make his apology to her in person and then he could explain every thing to her, including who Patricia was. So he said "My darling innocent Valerie, No body is going to come in between us in the future and you can stop worrying that Patricia is a competition to you at all. You would understand every thing when I tell you all in detail which I prefer to do in person. For the present just know that I love you with all my heart without any reservations." Then he added "You better be my girl for ever otherwise we Italians become unpredictable." he laughed and Valerie sensed the light heartedness and the bliss which matched her own.

"I will", was her reply.

" How is that you could write such a passionate letter but cannot talk more than two words on the phone?"

"I am speechless"

"You should become speechless only when I kiss you"

Valerie let out a giggle like a teenager. "I don't feel like cutting short but I must because I am calling from a public booth on my way to see my father. I simply couldn't wait till the evening to hear you darling, but unfortunately there are more than two people waiting to make a call and if I continue I might get clouted." Valerie laughed at his comment and said, "Well you better not" and he again said "I love you", and Valerie replied, "I love you too Quinn" this time every word was clear when he called her 'My darling' before he bade his sweet good bye.

Chapter 30

It took some time for Valerie to replace the receiver. She was in a sweet dream and every feature of her beautiful face showed the innocent bliss of love reflected with a flush, specially deepening her normally rosy cheeks. She bit her lower lip with a dreamy thought of Quinn's kisses it would receive when he came. She couldn't continue her work, neither she could sit and stare. Suddenly she wanted to shout and she wanted to dream, she wanted to laugh and she wanted to be with Quinn. Knowing that the last wish should wait for some time, she got up and went out of her room. Most of them were working seriously in the outer office and nun of them noticed her coming. She walked straight to Miss. Wagner's desk and said "Miss Wagner I would like to go early today, and if any calls come to me you could tell them I have gone home. Miss Wagner looked at her in surprise and then asked, "Are you alright Miss Wilson?" Torn between her dream world and her working world Valerie said "Yes of course. It's only that I received an unexpected message" "Is it regarding the Senior Patterchinni?" She was concerned. Valerie understood her anxiety and said, "He is making good progress and if every thing goes well Qui..."she bit her lip for the slip and added, "Mr. Patterchinni must be here in a few days time".

Miss Wagner showed her relief by letting out a sigh. Valerie, for no reason took Quinn's room keys and opened it just for the pleasure of going into it. Entering the room she looked round and saw a photo on his office table. She took it and gave a kiss and feeling shy for doing it she turned and ran towards the door. The moment she reached the door she checked herself before closing the door and tried to walk normally towards the entrance. But the swing of her hip and light in her eyes conveyed a lot. If at that moment Quinn had seen her he would have realised how much Valerie loved him. If at all any one believed in the seventh heaven then Valerie was right there now. She felt like talking to some one. But with whom? Her father or Sally would be the best but then she would wait till the evening so that they are definitely at home. Till then she would enjoy Berlin. Her car entered the 17th June Street where the Technical University was. There were big buildings and most of the people were in pairs. They were talking, kissing, and necking and unlike in England they have the freedom to do anything even in public places. Passers by did not seem to bother about what they saw. But for Valerie it was a new experience, and to her surprise every couple appeared to be herself and Quinn. Blushing at the thought she drove pass them and parked the car in a quiet place and thought about the new enchanting development in her life. How fate had brought her from England to Berlin to meet Quinn whose roots were in Italy. She often read that Berlin has a magic but she never thought that she would personally see that. How long she stayed there she had no idea but suddenly it was dark and she realised she should go back to her flat in case Quinn called her again.

How right she was. For when she entered her flat she heard the telephone. Quickly she ran to the telephone and it stopped ringing. Disappointed she went to the kitchen to make some coffee. That call never came back. Wondering whether to call Quinn or not she sat on the sofa. She simply wanted to dream, dream and dream. She felt shy to call Quinn so she closed her eyes thinking of Quinn. Something at the back of her mind told her that was not real but she ignored that. She thought about her father's reaction. Surely he would be delighted. Sally would be thrilled. How could she be so sure that he would propose to her and above all agree to have the marriage quickly. Her common sense warned her to wait till Quinn confirmed it in person. Her thoughts flew in another direction. What should she wear when he returned to Berlin. Should she run and hug him or stand still, till he made the first advance? Should she laugh, cry, smile or blush? She knew Quinn was not a kind of person who displayed his emotions easily. If he did then he did it with great effort.

She missed her father and Sally with whom she shared most of her feelings. She knew she would be shy when she saw Quinn. Wistfully she imagined his and her reactions. She resolved not to be over reactive, which she normally was and would wait and see what Quinn had to say before she committed herself fully. It was important to know what part this Patricia played in the whole story. If it was only a passing affair then she should be graceful enough to forgive and forget. If it was deeper than that still she must trust in him. The sincerity the passion, the love and the tenderness in his voice convinced her that his feelings were genuine.

Valerie did not know when she went to sleep for she saw dark clouds and rain and she was screaming and there was Quinn's troubled face, then she heard his carefree laugh, again there were dark shadows and then she heard thunder. She was half wake and half sleep when she heard big bangs on the bell and this time she realised it was not in her dreams but in her room. It took some time for her to fully recover from her trance and this time she really heard the bang on her doorbell. Some one was pressing it constantly that the whole room shrilled with the noise. She got up and went to the answering phone at the door and slowly asked "Who is that Please?" Somebody answered in an inaudible voice.

She could hear the heavy rain pouring out side. She pressed the button and waited at the door. Perhaps that young student who lived in the upper floor. Minutes ticked and then she heard her door bell, by now she was fully wake. She looked through the peep hole. She could see the drenched figure of Quinn. For a moment she couldn't move and the second ring made her to open the door. There stood a fully drenched Quinn with his hair plastered to his head his tie hanging pathetically, his face wet and drops of water hanging all over, with only a small travelling bag and his brief case. "Well do I have permission to enter?" Valerie got over from her initial shock, and plundered with delight, she realised that she was facing the man for whom she had given her heart totally.

Quinn was taking off his wet jacket and his shoes before he stepped in. Valerie's hand automatically stretched out and took the jacket and she turned to look for a hanger and there on the mirror she saw two people who were in love. A handsome man with water dripping face and a shy girl with dishevelled hair, crinkled dress half smudged lipstick mouth, half opened dress one ear ring missing, in other words a pathetic looking girl. She wanted to laugh but the sound didn't come out. All the planning she did for this meeting rolled in like a film.

And she turned to look at Quinn to see whether he was disappointed in what he saw. But to her surprise he was smiling and advancing towards her, saying "I imagined in all the possible way how you would look and adored them all, but this appearance never came across my mind. But to be frank this is the most wonderful appearance I have ever seen of you. Darling I love you and I can't stop loving you." Before she could speak any thing, he covered the distance in seconds while her heart thumbed madly and he cupped her upturned face, her voice failed and his lips trembled. Both of them were electrified and charged with desire. Unable to control himself Quinn bent and took her lips tenderly and passionately. This gesture made Valerie to lose her balance on the now wet carpet and brought her to the floor bringing down Quinn with her. Stunned by the physical impact they stared at each other and started to laugh." Slipping and falling are destined to accompany us" Quinn remarked as he propped himself against the wall. He hugged Valerie and drew her into his enormous chest. This time knowing the footing was firm he kissed her thoroughly and by the time he released her both of them were gasping for breath. Quinn found it delightful with the response he got from Valerie. And for Valerie it was simply divine happiness. The hunger in Quinn's eyes wanted more and Valerie was undecided. Quinn was so soft and gentle that she couldn't conceal her desire of wanting more. It was Quinn who broke the spell. "Valerie darling, You know I want as much as you want, but I always dreamed on having a beautiful wedding in the old church in which I grew up. Because I want to make my old man happy by having a quiet traditional ceremony before I touch you. You must be patient darling. Would you?". It was more like a begging to hide the fear that if Valerie says 'no' he was prepared to take her to bed now itself. Relishing the kisses Valerie looked at him into the eyes and said" I understand Darling, and I wish the same" Quinn got up first and pulled Valerie to her feet and said, "I am really cold. How about a drink. I think it is high time you give me one." Valerie laughed shyly and both of them walked towards the living room hand in hand.

It was past midnight before Quinn could bring the subject of Patricia into focus. Valerie was floating in the air and she half heard the name and nodded her head, paying little attention to what Quinn was saying. Suddenly the name Patricia rang the bell. And she asked quite light heartedly, "An old flame?" She was still smiling. Quinn gave an impression of giving the question some contemplation before replying, "No niece, my only living young family member, and for your information she is a beautiful child of ten." He looked at her and saw her open mouth and her widened eyes, for a moment he thought she had seen some thing behind him and turned to verify his suspicion. Finding nothing, he was convinced his message was the reason for her reaction. So he continued " Patricia is my only sister's daughter. ", he drew a deep breath before he added," Her mother was Gina Haward about whom you made a report in your television." Valerie simply froze. She missed her heart beat. A peculiar noise, half whimper and half choking escaped from her. Quinn expected a violent reaction, and this calmness gave him the courage to continue with the story. He did not hide anything. He was not looking at her but instead he looked out of the window. When he came to the point of how he loved her he turned and looked her. The horror stricken face of Valerie was the last thing he expected. He stopped in the middle of the sentence and asked "Valerie have I hurt you that much " When she did not answer he moved towards her to take her in his arms. Valerie got up from the sofa they were sitting and walked towards the window. She was horrified to find out who Quinn was and why she was employed. She could not believe that she who had been genuine in her feelings should have such a punishment. The sweet torment she had all these days was nothing compared to what she was suffering now. She felt as though she was cheated in an otherwise fair game. She felt humiliated and her self respect was stripped off to nakedness. Quinn had stopped talking but looked at her with expectation. Valerie only stared at the empty space as though the clock had stood still. The ghostly silence that followed was broken when Valerie let out a heart touching cry, and sat on the floor covering her face with both her hands. Quinn could not wait any longer. In two strides he reached her and touched her shoulders. That was the last straw for her." Quinn Please don't touch me. And please leave me alone ". Quinn slowly withdrew his hands and retraced his steps. He saw the tears running like a river and wetting her dress. It hurt him so much that he said " Valerie darling I love you with all my heart, please believe me "She turned and looked at him with her tear stained face and asked, "How could you"? Quinn could feel the pain penetrating his skin like thousands of arrows but he did not want to give up.

" I accept at the beginning I was very angry, because I believed that your report was the cause for Gina's death, but I think because I loved you from the beginning I could not hurt you"

"I don't follow your argument. Even now there is no positive proof that I was not the reason." "But Valerie I love you only god knows how much, and nothing else matters "Quinn did not want to mention Gina's letter, thinking it would worsen the matter. He wanted to convince her of his love.

"But any time you may accuse me when it suits you"

"Valerie you know I will never be unreasonable. Otherwise I wouldn't have declared my love to you' 'He begged her.

"But it is a shaky foundation to start a married life. I can't be living in terror everyday, thinking one day or the other you will accuse me of Gina's death.

"Valerie listen to me, I promise you I will never ever do that" he said that for he knew for sure that she was not the cause.

"Quinn only god knows how much I love you. And how much effort I needed to tell you that my body aches and my heart bleeds at this moment. Believe me every fibre of me wants to be with you. But I still have a clear brain. If I give in now I will be in eternal hell. Directly or indirectly the guilt will be between us. More than you it is going to haunt me till I die. Do you mean to say that staying married to the brother will ever erase the guilt I will be carrying? You know what Princess Diana told in one of the interviews. 'From the beginning we were three people in our marriage.' It will be the same. Gina will be always in between us, especially with Patricia to live with us. Think of the pain you will have, I will have and later on when Patricia grows up she will have. I want to live with these bitter sweet memories, than living in fear for the rest of my life." The long talk made her pant. She was physically and mentally exhausted.

"But Valerie darling I love you more than anything else and when I don't believe that, why should you. I knew half the story then because your boss told me the report was your initiation and he had nothing to do with it." Quinn turned the argument into a different direction fearing at any time he might break and tell about Gina's letter which would be a doom for the whole affair. At the present mood if the secret of the letter was revealed he would never ever have the chance to win her heart. She would think only after reading Gina's letter he was sure of his love and not before. This will give a dim look on his love he had for her. So he added " now I love you, for better or worse " He wanted to sound light hearted.

" Did he?" He saw Valerie had not paid any attention to what he was saying, but only thinking about the accusation. " Now how do I defend myself? Would you believe that I was forced to resign since there was a moral blackmail imposed on me. And I was personally instructed by my boss to do this report. I was simply pushed to do the report. No you won't, because I don't have any proof Quinn. I have only god and myself as witness". Valerie's eyes looked as though she was physically hurt." I will believe all what you say Valerie, because I believe you " saying that Quinn took a few steps and came near her not daring to touch her. She looked deep into his eyes, her eye balls rolling from one side to the other, telling him a thousand things. Then her lips trembled, the tears welling in the eyes stayed still on one side and dropped from the other. Quinn felt pins pricking his heart, he wanted to take her in his arm and kiss that beautiful face but some thing warned him that a hurt beyond cure could not heal when it was still raw. He said softly "Valerie Darling let us forget every thing and start from the beginning. And moreover Gina was my sister and not my girl friend."

" That's the very reason Quinn, because blood is thicker than water and I know how you loved your sister. That relationship cannot be changed where as love for many people is just an illusion. As for me it is not. It is life itself. I will love you and only you till I die. I loved you even before you loved me and then itself I trained myself for the worst. My memories will be sweet."

He held her hands and tried to draw her close, but Valerie pulled her hand and turned and looked into the darkness through the window. The moon was covered with dark clouds like her heart. When she turned, her eyes were dry but had lost its shine. She swallowed the air in the mouth bending her head slightly and closing her eyes. She spoke with a flat voice "Quinn would you mind leaving me alone and go to a hotel". Startled Quinn tried to say something. But Valerie shook her head and said "You owe me that". Except his father, nobody dismissed him in such a manner. He turned and looked at his opened bag, reached it, dumped the things and closed it. He took the receiver and ordered a taxi. He understood nothing he said now would be accepted or heard by Valerie. Perhaps things will look different in the day light, he only hoped. Valerie was leaning on the wall staring at the ceiling. An occasional tremble of the lips and the tears that dropped every time she closed her eyes were the only signs of life in her. For both Valerie and Quinn the waiting was a torture. As a last attempt Quinn said " Valerie", She only uttered the word "Please " and shook her head. And her eyes begged him not to talk further. The silence that invaded was so profound that each of them thought they heard their own heart beats. Never in his life was Quinn defeated like this. If he was to prove his love he had to be patient. Swallowing his pride he walked to the door with his bag. He heard a slight movement behind him and then his name "Quinn", he turned with a hope in his eyes, only to receive a harder blow, for Valerie said "Could you release me from my contract. I want to go home." For a moment he was lost for words, then as a last appeal he asked "Do you really want to?". She replied calmly " Yes, please". If she had been angry and shouted at him, he wouldn't have felt like that. But it was a punishment of torture. The elision of any definite feeling was shared by both of them. It was simply factitious. The emotions that were boiling in both their hearts were covered only by a feign. Wounded in heart, hurt in the soul, Valerie closed the door of her heart not only to Quinn but also to life itself. She was led to a mirage without being told it was a desert. One cannot be prudent as far as feelings are concerned. Now she stood alone in the middle of the desert. For the second time in her life fate played an unfair game.

Quinn always thought it was embarrassing to accept defeat. But here he was forced to accept defeat without any hope for a second chance. The droop on his shoulders was a clear indication of a defeat. He never wanted any thing more than what he wanted now. He wanted the love of Valerie, and he fully understood he cannot have that. Why was that he was successful in getting all what he wanted and the most important wish was grabbed away in minutes. Was it because he wanted to have a clean chest before he stepped into a commitment. Would it have been different if the truth was revealed at a later stage or not at all. They both loved each other that was clear. He would have argued his point if she was in a position to listen but she was not. Displaying such feelings beyond a certain limit was not manly. And that was the last thought in his mind when he answered with down cast eyes "If that is what you want, I will do that " With these words he opened the front door and went out not only closing the door of the flat, but also closing the most wonderful relationship, closing the great love he ever had. Only that door knew how he entered with vibrant love and left as a shattered man. Valerie stayed awake the rest of the night. She could feel the pain exceeding the power of endurance resulting in an empty feeling.

Chapter 31

That day when she was sitting in the plane alone, and no way of getting any kind of comfort was the worst thing in her life she thought. If at all there was something called the peak of sadness then she was experiencing that. Her heart bled with pain. The love that she cherished was offered and snatched away on the same day. Once she was reading a comment about Shaw's Pygmalion. It was described that Shaw ended the love of Elisa to say that 'if all love ended in happiness then it is a misfit to reality'. Now she realised how true it was. Love in her dictionary was something special - pure, blissful and spotless. When one of them was missing the beauty of it was lost. She could not accept nor reject Quinn's love. Only one question hung back. Why should people who live in hypocrisy and cheating were able to achieve their wishes and not people like her who believed in truth and sincerity. Here she was prepared to give every small portion of her heart, her absolute love and her entire life but saw that her castle of love simply tumbling down.

But then in her solitary confinement she asked one question. 'Do I love Quinn even if I can't live with him.? It was then that the great revelation first blinked and then came in wide screen.' Yes I love Quinn for better or worse 'and all the beautiful things flashed back hiding the only black hole of her love, the melancholy parting. It was far beyond the orbit. Then she knew she was strong enough to live with this love she had for Quinn. It was better to part when you were still in love than to part disappointed with the expectations. Sometimes marriages started with love and ended in hate. The mended marriages were not the same. Sometimes somewhere the brightness would be dimmed and then it would be a blind folded journey. There would be occasional breaks disrupting the continuity. What was the fun in losing and starting all over again. She wanted to taste the pure love and she had it. She was prepared to live with the past memories and dreams. She was sure whether she married Quinn or not he would be always a part of her. It would sound crazy for many people, but that was the truth. And 'Truth is stranger than fiction.' `Time may heal the wound´ people said, but as far as Valerie was concerned, time would stand still, the love would be there, Quinn would be in her heart, memories would be vivid and the wound would be raw. She would live with these knowing without any doubt she could continue to live with the same love for Quinn but this time without expectations.

****

The plane was in the run way, and in a few minutes it would come to a halt and the passengers would disembark and so would Valerie. It was four years since she left this very same airport with a heavy heart, promising never to come back and shook the dust off. But time changes and people do change to a certain extent. The initial vehemence changes into frustration and ends up in acceptance, allowing all the previous determinations to fall down into a pit with only one standard saying 'life must go on'. The blow ups often boil down. The wrath boils down to anger which leads to reason which in turn ends in philosophy.

Four years ago Valerie had a clean break from relationships and carried only the feelings, dreams and all other logic connected to love in her heart. As a teenager she was fierce and independent. She had an inner conflict about falling in love. May be she read too many romances that she started to disbelieve in the existence of love itself. Her first novel was the " Cloister and the Hart " by Sir. Walter Scott recommended by her father who was an ardent fan of Walter Scott. But unfortunately it developed a weird feeling about love. She could not understand how two people who loved each other could ever live with another person and when they had a chance to come together how could he refuse and continue to live in a monastery. Either love did not exist or moral was hypocrisy. When she read Dumas' 'The Count of Montecresto' she refused to believe that love could bring revenge in Edmond's heart or the love of Mercedes was no more there in her heart because he had changed. Or why Romeo from Shakespeare believed he loved Roselin which was thought immoral and found love different when he met Juliet, and ended up with a tragic death. When grievances add up they become more powerful. She became too emotionally charged to deal with it effectively. At last she gave up rejecting all plausible reasoning of love as ' nothing other than selfish motives with temporary stability and a satisfaction of having victory over another human being. 'The more she thought the more clouded the message became. Therefore love became an askance in her dictionary.

All these were before she met Quinn. Then things became different. At the beginning Quinn was simply trespassing her path. But small incidents added glamour to that. Then she realised that her formidable power of resistance was slowly melting away, and the power of love invading her heart and started to dominate her. All these happened long before she noticed Quinn 's attention turning towards her. Women like men, admire those who are stronger. And Quinn was strong. At the beginning she trusted on feminine instinct in particular, and found both she and Quinn thought the same thing at the same time. Often she was about to tell 'I think and you voice it' when her thoughts and his thoughts were exactly the same. She admired that maddening self assurance he had in making decisions. Unlike Hans who evaded a direct answer by his impetuous bullying, Quinn always gave straight forward answers. Although they sounded rude at times never offended any one. In a way Valerie loved the combination of strength and roughness with a charm that prostrated and the domineering superiority. No one hates a baby for its ineptitudes she argued. Radiance of these revelations resulted in a dazzling impression and it slowly took complete grip of her. At first she tried to erase these feelings as ' romantic notions' and could have succeeded ' if romance were not so deeply ingrained in human nature'. Her love had a noble passion. She had no idea who Patricia was but always lived in her own world where no body else existed other than herself and Quinn. She was surprised to find she was love sick like a teenager. She tried to conciliate on the fact with disastrous results. She knew these gushing desires may one day end up in unbearable humiliation. But she couldn't come out of it. She had her secret mischievous moments before, but when this became serious, and fearing that others may discover, she built a pussy foot around her feelings, and every thing looked normal from the outside. One advantage was that she did not have many friends in Berlin and the other was no man had a chance to enter her heart as long as Quinn was in the vicinity. Quinn's behaviour in different circumstances developed a thrill in her life. Enjoying and interpreting each of them became her daily task. She was happy that she wrote the entries on special days voicing her interpretation and when she was at a dead- end left it open. She was attracted by his never failing affection, care and attention she never received before. But soon she realised, to wish and to have are two different things. She was instinctively aware of the charm that prostrated in Quinn, and was slowly drawn into the web of love. But she felt that this love was different. Because she knew at any time she could face a disappointment for she had no idea what or how Quinn felt. The only thing that she did not want to happen was humiliation. She was safe as long as she was within close doors. All her tender recollections were penned and not voiced. She was glad about it now. The tightening of the chest, the frustration, the torture, the sadness, the pain, the detachment to life, the tears, and all such feelings one had when there was a love failure awakened a suspicion of truth. A truth that she never heard or knew. It brought a tranquillity she had never experienced. Her heart was filled with the bliss of pure love. A love with which she could live without regrets. She lived with those beautiful moments she had with Quinn. After four years she still had the same love and it never faltered. A love without selfishness, a love that was eternal, a love that had changed her to face and accept any other situation. Her pure love was so pronounced even without seeing Quinn, it gave her the strength. It gave her the ethics of life-never to hurt any one, never to hang on to hate, never to be influenced by anger or take revenge. Because hate crushed love, anger destroyed the spirit and 'vengeance was a lazy method to get over the grief´. And now she lived with Quinn in her own special way. She was sure such experience of love was not shared by many people. But she was convinced. She remembered Oscar Wilde saying `Marriage is the ethics of the conservatives´, but she knew ` love is the ethics of the universe´. Love may not always end in a union though. Pure love should stay as pure love till God, fate or nature decides to end it by taking us away from this life. When she reached this maturity she was not afraid to come back to Berlin or even to meet Quinn.

Chapter 32

Although this was the first time Valerie was attending the 'Berlinale', The International film festival- Berlin was not new to her. Except for a few changes it was the same old Berlin. She had booked a room in Hotel Hyatt where the press conferences for various films would take place. The competition films were to be screened at the Berliner Palast in Potsdammer P1atz. New constructions, attractive architecture and building complexes of well known companies like Sony and Daimler Chrysler had replaced a one time bushes and ruins. Especially during the festival season the place became busier. Big attractive posters were pasted all over the area. The eyes of Jacky Chan held a humour, Nicole Kidman was staring straight, the dimple of Catherine Zeta Jones, the unmistakable nose of Matt Demon, and Gwyneth Paltrow in the nineteenth century dress and was that Johnny Deep behind that. One poster caught her eyes very much. The Talent Contest poster carried the slogan ` Wish I could edit life as well´. Valerie was sure that would have been the wish of all. She was absorbed in those posters when she felt somebody pushing her and she turned to see the sign "PRESS" with an arrow pointing upwards. Remembering her accreditation she moved with the crowd. It was frustrating to see the slow speed at which the line of journalists was moving. There were only two people at the counter and four at the other. But there were a lot of formalities to be finished before one could reach the counter to collect the badge. Some one was complaining about the delay, and another answered "Thank your stars you are not in Cannes, where things are chaotic." Valerie only smiled. You could hear German, English, French, Spanish and many other languages spoken. There were recognitions, greetings, complains, information, questions and answers all at the same time. There were various hand bills and booklets for them to pick and choose. Valerie took a few and scanned through them to forget the boredom. At last she reached the counter and collected her badge together with the catalogue. She pushed the badge in her hand bag so that she could take it easily and put the rest of the materials in her day bag. She had not paid much attention on the competition films for she was doing a report mainly on documentary films. Since most of the programmes started the next day she decided to see the opening film without paying much attention to the details of the film. In festivals like this you move with the crowd on the first day, then only you organise yourself, because of the formalities, setting the whereabouts and confusion on the whole. No wonder Valerie was caught in the same web. The first press screening was at Two O' Clock. She had to hurry if she were to see the film. What with three thousand odd journalists attending. One may never know when the theatre is full and when not. She rushed to the Berliner Palast only to be halted by the red jacketed assistant who informed her there was another ten minutes to go. Crowd started to gather and when the time came, they all wanted to go at the same time. She felt as though she was at the high school waiting to go out after the assembly. Such a rush, such a push.

The film started after a slight delay. Titles were running and then came the bolt from the blue. The bold letters fell on the screen, 'Produced by Quinn Patterchinni.' The name stayed only for a few seconds but for Valerie it stayed for ever. She could not concentrate much on the film any further. It was news for her but not a surprise. It brought all the memories. After four years of determination she really wanted to see him not out of weakness but to test herself. The only contact she got was the letter that arrived cancelling her contract posted from her London office. Not once he tried to call her. Two years ago she saw his marriage announcement on the papers. She only knew that his bride to be was a rich Italian girl, not in any way connected to the film world. Occasionally she saw his photographs on the news papers or alive on some television reports about VIPs. She always remembered those beautiful moments she had and tried to live with them.

Valerie's heart pained for an unknown reason. Some time back she read these words about love. "The fortunate thing in love is to love some one and not to be loved by some one". It reminded another phrase "To be loved and to return love is human, but to love without expectation is angelic". Not all could reach such maturity. For many of them it sounded preposterous. But a few who experienced would know the peace and happiness they had in doing so. She had almost reached a third of her life span and she could still see the starting point vaguely and she could not predict how it will end. The sweet memory of her love was the most wonderful thing that had happened to her although in weak moments she cried. She never wanted to talk about them because her memories were personal and precious. There was no purpose in trying to explain to others, either they would laugh or reserve judgement but never understand. Love is an experience you feel and not a mathematical calculation.

Valerie had smiled at the expression "Love is a healthy sickness". Isn't it ironic that different people had different feelings about the same concept. Did it mean definitions given were more of a personal view than definition itself. May be technical terms had fixed definitions but not the feelings. For Shaw love was a phase in life, for Scott a marvellous feeling, for Dumas it could end in vengeance, and for Tolstoy it was passion. They saw it only from one angle. The only plausible explanation was given by Oscar Wilde when he said "Life is a sacrament and love is its ideal". But in Valerie's dictionary, `Love does not boasts, it is not arrogant, does not commit injustice, does not get annoyed, does not think of evil, rejoices in the truth, it trusts, it never fails and it stays for ever without any expectations´. One may be reminded of the bible. But this was Valerie's code of love. A person like Hans could not understand for he was a sadist and Quinn could not understand because he was a conqueror.

She knew Quinn was outraged when she refused his offer. How simple it would have been just to marry Quinn and settle down in life like every other lover. But she couldn't. Quinn was cynical she did not hate him, he was moody she did not mind, he was mean she was not angry, he was unreasonable she was not disgusted. She simply loved him with all his moods. There was no change in her love. For Valerie, love was not just a passionate commitment with the aim of marriage for a routine life. For her, love was an unknown yearning for an unexplained feeling. It was simply the enlightenment of purity. Its recognition itself gave happiness. It could not survive with a seed of doubt. A scar could not be hidden, a tear could not vanish, they could only be mended without a guarantee. Valerie could bear the separation but could never endure disappointment. For separation increased love and disappointment destroyed love. Valerie wanted her love to live.

Somebody stepped on her foot. The theatre was still dark since the film had not yet finished. But people were leaving, probably to get a seat at the press conference hall. Valerie got up. Something in her pushed her and she walked out of the theatre bending her head so that the others were not disturbed when she came out. Outside it was still day light and her eyes took sometime to adjust to the surroundings. She blinked and walked towards the side entrance of Hotel Hyatt. The hall was already half full with journalists and the TV cameras were parked at the end of the hall. Translating equipments were at one end. The seats were arranged in a crest formation, with the film banners at the back of the podium. Valerie took a seat next to the aisle. She read the names of the participants. Quinn's name was there at the extreme corner. A slight cold stream went through her blood, then her face softened, she waited for the moment with mixed emotions. He might not recognise her in this crowd. That did not hurt her. she was delighted to see him, to see the changes in him, to refresh her memory for a later day, as though collecting new photographs for a biography.

There were flashes at the entrance, announcing the arrival of the participants. The actors and actress were gliding with the typical style, there were hundreds of photographs taken by different press photographers at different angles, most of them were standing on their seats hiding the whole view and Valerie strained her neck to see the podium but was unsuccessful. At last all the excitement ended and the guests settled them selves and the photographers too. Valerie saw all of them and to her disappointment Quinn's seat was empty. Something in her died. Then she saw him walking to the podium and taking his seat. He looked different. There was a modern beard and a moustache. He was wearing a suite without a tie, and looked more casual than formal. There was a slight stoop when he was sitting and he was parting the moustache and stroking it occasionally while listening to the others. A new addition to his appearance. He was measuring the crowd and then his eyes met Valerie's. His eyes narrowed as though he was making sure what he saw were true. Valerie's eyes carried the same love and softness. His eyes wavered a little as though if he looked else where she might vanish.

The press conference had just started, and it would go on at least for half an hour. She saw him signing one of the assistants and when he came and bent he said something to him while the assistant scanned through the crowd and stopped on Valerie's face. Then he returned with a glass of cola and a piece of paper. Quinn wrote something and gave it to him. There was a question for him from a journalist while he finished writing. He answered calmly and he never looked in her direction, implying the recognition was only for a fleeting second. Valerie tried to concentrate on the conference, but her heart was racing so fast she had to hold the chair for support. She wanted to go out but her legs wouldn't move. She closed her eyes for a moment and she felt a hand on her shoulder. Her head half turned to make sure, and seeing the hand of the assistant she had a peculiar feeling in the stomach. There was a piece of paper folded into two, stretched before her eyes. Her right hand bent across her face to get that note. A few people gave a side glance but nun of them took it seriously. These things were quite common in places like these. She slowly opened the note. Her hands were trembling. There were only two lines. " Please meet me at Hotel Kempensky at 8 today. I will be waiting for you. Quinn".

When she read the note she raised her eyes to look at him. The same hypnotic eyes stared at her, bringing out the memories. Those eyes waited for an answer. Valerie closed her eyes to show her consent. Press conference proceeded with a few questions for the producer. Quinn answered them without any 'trying to impress' tactics. He spoke precisely and to the point and never tried to bully the young journalists for their superficial questions. It was funny that hundreds of journalists sit but only a few asked questions and half of them were stupid questions. They used the most unusual words with a peculiar word order not used in the English language. One question was so long that at the end of the question the actor said "Madame, I do not understand your language". Valerie suppressed a smile and saw Quinn putting his tongue to his cheek while the others smiled and the young lady sat down with embarrassment. By the time the presenter said "Thank you" and escorted the team out of the podium it was half past six.

Valerie returned to her room, still pondering on her reaction seeing Quinn after a long time. She could only confirm her love was like an eternal flame with the same force and ardour with an exception. Now she had no expectations. With this confidence she prepared herself to meet Quinn. She was beautiful as ever with that black dress, the reflection on the mirror spoke the truth. She took care of her appearance not to seduce any one especially Quinn, for that was never her intention, but she thought it was necessary because Hotel Kempensky was the place most of the Hollywood stars stayed and she dared not discredit Quinn the Hollywood Producer when she visited him as his guest. She arrived at quarter to eight and approached the reception. When she told her name he immediately recognised but something told her that Quinn was there in the room. Automatically her head turned to the stairs and saw him coming down the stairs. He crossed the hall swiftly only with a few strides stretching his hand to her and his other hand barely touching her shoulders. He escorted her towards the chairs. Seeing her discomfort he asked "Or would you prefer to go to my suite, where we could talk", there was a tint of hesitancy as though he was sceptic about the idea. She smiled and said, "As you please, I don't mind". If he was astonished by her answer he cleverly hid it by adding "Then come this way". He walked to the lift and pressed the button to the second floor. He led her through the velvet carpeted passage, opened his suite and allowed her to enter first. He got her coat and hung it and led her to the sofa in the living room, settled her on the sofa and he himself took the next one and sat down. He called the room service and looked at her "Tea or coffee?" "Tea please" He ordered coffee for him. So he did not change his habit. Valerie's emotions were well under control. Some thing she had disciplined herself for the past four years. Both were silent for some time. Then both started at the same time "How…" and stopped. Quinn grinned. Valerie took the initiative to continue the conversation.

"I half expected to see you though I had no idea you are a film producer".

"Well, this is my first film"

"Oh I see, What do you expect, acceptance or an award?"

"I don't know, maybe both"

Then it stuck him 'Why the hell we are formal´, so he asked, " What are you doing now Valerie?"." I am a sub editor for…," she mentioned a popular magazine, "and a lecturer at the film Institute"

"Satisfied with the job?"

"Oh yes, quite a challenge I should say" There was silence again. Then unable to continue the pretence Quinn said "I thought you would contact me and waited for more than two years"

"Well we decided on something and I kept it". He frowned and looked at her as though he did not understand and then said "I am married now".

"I know that, I read it on the papers." Quinn could not wait any longer "How are you Valerie?", automatically he glanced at her left hand. "No I am not married. I could not forget you". "Then why did you keep quiet?", there was annoyance in his voice.

"Because I could only love you, but I couldn't marry you. And there was no point in giving false hope".

"Valerie it pains my heart. I wanted to punish myself often, but did not know how".

"Quinn please don't hurt me by saying that. I never wished, even in my dreams, to make you unhappy. That was the main reason I did not contact you all these years".

"How is it possible. Day and night I was tortured"

"Please don't. Do you know all these four years I lived with your memory. Once I got over the shock, I realised I loved you and you only. When ever I wanted to talk with you I simply write an entry in my note book. Good times and bad times."

"But is that enough?"

"I think I accepted what I can't get, and tried to live with that. I clearly understood if all of us get what we wish then that is not reality".

"But why you Valerie?"

"May be trials are given to those of us who could bear".

"Since when did you become a preacher". Valerie sensed his frustration in that question and allowed the silence to answer him. At last he said "At least I want you to see this for my peace of mind" and he got up and brought the lap top.

There was a knock on the door at the same time a voice said "Room service". Quinn got up and opened the door. Both were silent till the room boy left the place. Quinn poured her tea and his coffee, left it on the table and looking at her directly said "Valerie I want to show you Gina's letter written just before she died" His fingers were working on the system. At last he just pressed the button and turned the monitor in her direction. Valerie read the letter in silence and continued to be silent. Then she looked at Quinn and asked "Did you know about this letter then?"

"Yes"

"Before or after you proposed to me"

"Before"

"You loved me knowing about this letter"

"No, I loved you before I read the letter"

"Thank you Quinn for telling the truth"

Then she looked at Quinn with extraordinary calmness before she added "We can only wish certain things, we can't realise them. Some people say it's god's will and the others say it's the fate. What ever it is, the truth remains that not all our wishes come true, regardless how genuine they are".

"You were adamant not I".

Valerie laughed and said "I was adamant not to marry you, I never denied my love"

"Is it enough?", Quinn lifted his head and turned it to an angle expressing his hidden anger.

"You know Quinn, I have often wondered why Jane Austin who could write such passionate love stories never married. Now I know. She must have loved a person whom she could not marry. That's why her stories always had happy endings. What she did not have in reality she had it in her stories and enjoyed them. The love like hers and mine happens only for a few". Quinn looked at her, refusing to believe her arguments, but did not utter a word. Valerie was forced to continue in order to convince him.

"Religion should not be mocked at as hypocrisy, therefore I did not join the monastery, and the strength of true love upholds you and not weakens you therefore I did not commit suicide. I would like to live and prove my love, for it is not sympathy I am looking for, it is the acceptance of true love till death do us part."

"How could you be happy?", Quinn asked this question not convinced with her argument,

"I analysed this for the past four years and the same answer comes over and over again", she looked through the window as though `the answer was blowing in the wind´.

Quinn looked at her and closed his eyes wanting to hear her talking so that at one point he could find to accept what she was telling. Then he heard her continue, "When one of the partners die many of them say they will live with the memory and had done so. That is a fantasy. My argument is more of reality. I will live with the memory of the living person whom I could see and talk. Doesn't it sound logical" Quinn suddenly opened his eyes and looked at her in wonder, realising her argument really had its logic. Perhaps it had brought a new philosophy. He had no words to say. Encouraged by his silence Valerie continued" Quinn you are married and you have a duty to your family. Please don't worry about me. I have chosen how I want my life and you yours. Our paths should not cross often, but who knows it may, and when that happens we should feel happy at least we could see each other. I am happy I found the love that I always thought never existed. I should be happy that you really loved me. I was not fortunate enough to have you. That's all"

"Valerie I want to know whether you are angry, and if I had hurt you what should I do?"

"I knew you tried your best to amend. It was true, at the beginning I was hurt beyond repairs. Only I and my bed knew the amount of tears I shed. But then I realised I should come out of it, if I am to make your life happy, and I did, for tears will hinder your loved ones happiness". She paused to think about the sleepless nights and the endless tears she shed before she got back her balance. The expression on Quinn's face was unexplainable. Noticing that, she brought a smile to her face and blinked away the tears that was about to drop. She desperately fought and won. To hurt Quinn was the last thing she wanted.

"Valerie if only..." Quinn started and stopped for he had nothing to offer and he became cognizant that some things are done too late and some decisions are made too late and some wishes may never happen. Valerie cleared her throat, half expecting him to look away from her. No he was just gazing at her with tenterhooks for a consolation he might have in the future.

There was an angelic calmness on Valerie's face when she said," Quinn, all the happy moments I still carry. They are pleasant. They are beautiful and they are for ever. It is true I cry sometimes for no reason, and these wonderful memories cheer me up. I have long forgotten expectations. Some people are always lucky some people are sometimes lucky and only a few are never lucky. I think I am one of them." She looked at him for a reaction, and when he did not she continued," I came to your suite knowing very well that I am strong and I have proved that to you. No other man can ever stir my emotions as long as I live." The silence in the room spoke the rest of the feelings of those two hearts.

The phone shrilled and brought both of them to their senses. Quinn lifted the receiver and pressed the button to give an engaged sound. Valerie said " I think its time for me to go" She got up and reached for her coat. When Quinn came to help her she refused politely. At least she said what she wanted to say, whereas Quinn never said anything. He had sealed his lips, closed the door of his heart not only to Valerie but also to the whole world. No body knew what was in his heart. He buried his feelings deep into the darkness of the memory where no man could ever reach them.

Valerie never asked `Why did he marry´ and he never said at least he made his father happy by obliging his wish.

At the door Valerie turned and said "Please don't come with me. Parting will be difficult in a public place. Please allow me to hold your hand a few moments for me to carry the memory with me. Because they are going to accompany me till the end."

Quinn gave his hand and first time in his life his hands were shaking. Valerie's mouth smiled while her eyes pleaded not to feel sorry for her. Her eyes closed for a moment and two warm tear drops fell on the hands. She turned and walked towards the lift with tears blurring her vision. Was it happiness or sadness no one knew.

****

We readers have the chance to read Valerie's last entry.

> *Quinn my love, I know what you feel and I know how you feel, because I know what true love is. Life is a journey with junctions and curves. At the junctions we may take different directions but at the curves we may fall or escape. The former is failure and the latter is success. I failed. I am not a coward to become weak. I am only a human who knows when to cry and*

*when to laugh. The reason is either too much joy or too much sadness. But
when I cry I think it is joy. I can only say*
In your language

Que Sera Sera

And in mine

What ever will be will be.